TWISTED TALES

INFAMOUS TALES

Edited By Briony Kearney

First published in Great Britain in 2022 by:

Young Writers
Remus House
Coltsfoot Drive
Peterborough
PE2 9BF
Telephone: 01733 890066
Website: www.youngwriters.co.uk

Printed and bound in the UK by BookPrintingUK
Website: www.bookprintinguk.com
YB0504M

FOREWORD

Welcome, Reader!

Come into our lair, there's really nothing to fear. You may have heard bad things about the villains within these pages, but there's more to their stories than you might think...

For our latest competition, Twisted Tales, we challenged secondary school students to write a story in just 100 words that shows us another side to the traditional storybook villain. We asked them to look beyond the evil escapades and tell a story that shows a bad guy or girl in a new light. They were given optional story starters for a spark of inspiration, and could focus on their motivation, back story, or even what they get up to in their downtime!

And that's exactly what the authors in this anthology have done, giving us some unique new insights into those we usually consider the villain of the piece. The result is a thrilling and absorbing collection of stories written in a variety of styles, and it's a testament to the creativity of these young authors.

Here at Young Writers it's our aim to inspire the next generation and instill in them a love of creative writing, and what better way than to see their work in print? The imagination and skill within these pages are proof that we might just be achieving that aim! Congratulations to each of these fantastic authors.

CONTENTS

Aylesford School, Aylesford

Miley Simpson (11)   1
Isabel Rutter   2
Freddie Holmes   3
Jessica Williams (11)   4

Cokethorpe School, Witney

Sam Farr (14)   5

Higham Lane School Business And Enterprise College, Nuneaton

Katie Gavan (15)   6
Kaidence Whitmore (14)   7

Holbrook Academy, Holbrook

Summer Wynn-Blackburn (13)   8
Aliesha Ranson   9
Amelia Bloomfiled (15)   10
James Pook (13)   11
Miles Marazzi (16)   12
Lilly-Mai King (14)   13
Molly Alice Wainwright (14)   14
Lillie Howlett (11)   15

Holmleigh Park High School, Tuffley

Erin May Jarratt (11)   16
Eloise Medd (12)   17
Jac Griffiths   18

Holyport College, Holyport

Leonie Trinh (11)   19

Madani Girls' School, Whitechapel

Hela Nikben (14)   20

Poplar Adolescent Unit, Rochford

Caitlin Pujol (17)   21

Purbrook Park School, Purbrook

Harrison Baxter   22

Solihull Sixth Form College, Solihull

Talha Ajaz (16)   23
Aishah Begum (16)   24

Springboard Education, Lancing

Stan Seaman   25

St Killian's College, Carnlough

Alfie Morrow (11)   26
Maggie Steele (12)   27
Abigail Morrow (11)   28

St Louise's Comprehensive College, Belfast

Naoise Murphy (12)	29
Jamey Holland (13)	30
Nikita Carlin	31
Jackson O'Riordan (12)	32
Eve Rose Maguire (13)	33
Lana Sutcliffe (13)	34

St Mark's West Essex Catholic School, Harlow

Lucy Wood (12)	35
Finley Sweeting (11)	36

St Michael's CE High School, Chorley

Maisie Preston (12)	37

St Robert Of Newminster, Fatfield

Kosi Onwuneme (12)	38
Sam Green (12)	39
Lucy Lodge (13)	40
Neyatha Vinoy	41
Ronnie Chan (13)	42

St Thomas More RC Academy, North Shields

Tilly Milner (14)	43
Evie Race (11)	44
Gracie Davis (15)	45
Sophia Dodds (11)	46

St Thomas The Apostle College, Nunhead

Thomas Baars	47

Stirling High School, Stirling

Eva Richards (13)	48

Stockport School, Stockport

Izzy W	49

Swanlea School, Whitechapel

Adiba Rahman (11)	50
Ruqayyah Chowdhury	51
Afreen Khan (12)	52

Sydney Russell School, Dagenham

Ruth Ogbuokiri (13)	53
Elisa Gjoka (13)	54
Kevin Gjoka (12)	55

The Costello School, Basingstoke

Freddie Clarke (11)	56
Jasmina Mackowiak (12)	57
Natasza Wijata (11)	58
Meggy Meng (12)	59
Amaya O'Sullivan (11)	60
Stan Trussler (11)	61
Jess Croxon (11)	62
Josh Somerville (12)	63
Rakshit Saravanakumar (11)	64
Ana Patel-Potter (11)	65
Max Huang (11)	66
Leon Hynan (12)	67
Charleigh Connoley (11)	68
Holly Wolldridge (11)	69
James Ennis (12)	70
Immy Kane (11)	71
Charlie McLoughlin (12)	72
Saira Shrestha (11)	73
Ethan Spurway (12)	74
Kashish Ghale (11)	75
Nicole Villavicencio Duran (11)	76
Alex West (11)	77

Olly Tavendale (11)	78
Magi Kasabova (11)	79
Brooke Olive (11)	80
Ameliah Ward (11)	81
Chloe Millard (11)	82
Elliot Wilson (11)	83
Isla Waugh-Bacchus (11)	84
Giacomo Sordon (12)	85
Julia Borowczyk (11)	86
Caitlin Mutlow (11)	87
Ryan Tillotson (12)	88
Jeron Thottungal (11)	89
Addi Beaumont (12)	90

The FitzWimarc School, Rayleigh

Sydney Dukelow-Saxon (14)	91
Khira Robinson (12)	92
Charlotte Kelleher (13)	93
Lorna Quince (14)	94
Tristan Barker (14)	95
Aimee Moores (12)	96
Zoe Webb (14)	97
Luke Gould (13)	98
Brendon Pasipangodya (12)	99
Brooke Nicole Webb (13)	100
Reece Cooper (12)	101
Freya Bourdon (13)	102
Taya Evans (12)	103
Amy Gould (13)	104
Evie Francis (12)	105
Emily Duckworth (11)	106
Anna Louise Reynolds (16)	107
Billy Jay (12)	108
Emilia Agathangelou (13)	109

The Fulham Boys School, London

Theo Johnston (12)	110
Hamza Rhouzzal (12)	111
Rufus Dixon (12)	112
Will George (12)	113

The King's School, Worcester

Izzy Roberts (13)	114
Tom Phillips (13)	115
Sophie Evans	116
Sophie Ruane (13)	117

The Madani Academy, Buckland

Maariyah Naseem (12)	118
Jannah Alam (15)	119
Afifa (12)	120
Amani (14)	121
Nayyara Islam (12)	122

The Roseland Academy, Tregony

Kayna Farrell (13)	123

The Whitstable School, Kent

Reece Thwaites	124
Phoebe McLean	125
Líadain Saxe-Traquair (12)	126

The William De Ferrers School, South Woodham Ferrers

Ruby Booth	127
Toby Booth	128
Evie Booth	129
Amber Carver (14)	130
Maisie Smith (14)	131

The Wren School, Reading

Michele Abbey (12)	132
Mia Knox-Roberts (11)	133
Amal Nirmalkumar (11) & Fernando Ogbonna	134
Logan Codling (11)	135
Admiah Sinclair (11)	136
Elvie Oakland (11)	137

Thornhill Community Academy, Thornhill

Luke Winrow (12)	138
Amber Norman	139
Aamirah Maniar (11)	140
Summer Fox (11)	141
Sumayyah Hussain (14)	142
Janos Tauz (11)	143
Daisy Bramley (12)	144
Olivia Wilson (13)	145
Faye Longley (12)	146

Thorp Academy, Ryton

Martha Tweddell (12)	147
Evan Casson (11)	148
Isabel McGuire (13)	149
Eva Bainbridge (13)	150
Tiffany Bisset (13)	151

Tower Learning Centre Independent School, Blackpool

Elyssa Campbell	152

Towers School & Sixth Form Centre, Kennington

Imani Owade (13)	153
Amber Kennedy (13)	154
Shiloh Villion (13)	155
Penny Williams	156
Katie Woods	157
Karis Davies (13)	158
Molly James (11)	159
Gracie Hopper (14)	160

Trinity Academy Grammar, Sowerby Bridge

Imani Waseem (14)	161
Eleanor Baines (14)	162
Nusayba Zaman (13)	163
Amelia Czapiewska (14)	164

Aliya Rahman (13)	165
Karlina Buse (11)	166
Kamran Azam (14)	167

Trinity Academy Halifax, Holmfield

Kegan Bell (13)	168
Rowan Adam Aspin (16)	169
Katie McEvoy (15)	170
Yaseen Sakallah (14)	171
Axel Rivers (14)	172
Keeley Hambrey (13)	173
Julia Gonera (13)	174
Chanelle Clutton (13)	175
Haarisah Ideson (12)	176
Libby Condie (12)	177
Ferne Oxlade (12)	178
Lola Carney Williams (13)	179
Callum McDoanld (12)	180

Weaverham High School, Weaverham

Ruby-Jo Starkey (11)	181

Winchmore School, Winchmore Hill

Chanae Mcdonald (16)	182

THE
STORIES

BUDDY AND THE TENNIS BALL

Buddy, the Aylesford School dog, ran happily across the field, chasing his tennis ball ecstatically. Suddenly, the ball turned around. To Buddy's surprise, it opened its mouth, enlarged and roared at him, before heading towards the school.

Buddy snarled, running as fast as he could. He leapt in front of the ball and showed his teeth. The ball backed away slowly, shrinking as the proud dog protected his beloved school.

Luckily, the tennis ball had retreated and Buddy the Aylesford School dog had saved the school! Buddy barked happily, resuming leaping after his not-so-clean tennis ball.

Miley Simpson (11)
Aylesford School, Aylesford

THE ARIEL-5000 DISASTER

Everyone was at Mr Small's opening day to buy the newest computer there was. The Ariel-5000! Later that day, when all the computers were sold out, Mr Small began his evil plans. He hacked the system, put on his goggles, and hypnotised everyone in the city.

Mr Small ordered everyone to his trap and locked them all in their separate bubbles, floating through the sky. But something went wrong.

Bang! Crash! Thud! Everyone was trying to punch and kick their way out. Then Mr Small set off a smoke bomb and they all fell fast asleep. Would they survive?

Isabel Rutter
Aylesford School, Aylesford

LITTLE RED

It all started when Little Red Riding Hood walked into her grandma's house.

"Oh, please could you get your gran's medicine?" she said when Little Red Riding Hood went into the kitchen.

She put some cyanide into Gran's soup. Riding Hood gave Grandma her soup and Gran went into agonising pain and slowly died. Then Riding Hood stuffed her into a bag and dragged the bag out to the wolf.

As she turned around, she saw the wolf licking his lips. Riding Hood gave him the body and the wolf gave her a 500-pound note.

Freddie Holmes

Aylesford School, Aylesford

THE BOY

I moved to a new country: America. New home, new work, new life. I loved it there, it couldn't get any better!
But there was something there with me, I wasn't alone. It kept me up all night, I was scared. I went to work and told my workmates, they told me to get a priest but I refused because it had not done anything.
I got home, I heard noises coming from the basement. It was screaming, a little boy screaming. It was coming for me. I saw it running... What could I do? I stood there...

Jessica Williams (11)
Aylesford School, Aylesford

THE GREATEST TRAGEDY OF ALL

It is done. Yet as I stood alone, I was emotionless. No feeling of exultation even briefly came over me. What if, when we acknowledged the setting sun every night, pondering what we're most scared of losing, instead, we pondered what to do when we have won?

That, I fear, is the greatest tragedy of all. My brain, so fixed on achieving the ultimate goal, what came after never seemed to matter, and now, exhaustion enclosed me like a cocoon.

My breath shallowed and quickened simultaneously and I collapsed onto the floor, head in hands, tears slipping down my cheeks.

Sam Farr (14)
Cokethorpe School, Witney

I DON'T WANT TO HAVE TO KILL AGAIN

I don't want to have to kill again. Day after day, countless bodies pass through my jaws. I kill them. That's just what I do. It's what I've always done. I've never really thought about it until now.

Another body slides towards me. It makes a faint, weak rustle. Is it scared? I don't care. I can't care. If I care, I won't be able to finish the job.

My silvery teeth slash at its thin frame. One cut is all I need. It's all I ever need. It's done. A lone piece of paper slides out of the guillotine.

Katie Gavan (15)

Higham Lane School Business And Enterprise College, Nuneaton

THE BEGINNING OF THE END OF CHRISTMAS

Finally, I was about to win. I laughed with sinfulness. I wanted to steal everyone's happiness for Christmas, as Christmas was the worst thing that happened every year. I started with the adults as they were the hardest to take away. Then I began with the children. I dressed up as Santa Claus and began to set things on fire in front of them. Then they began to cry and scream.

It made me full of greatness and evilness. I ran away as fast as I could to escape tragedy. But I laughed wickedly the whole way. I was alive!

Kaidence Whitmore (14)

Higham Lane School Business And Enterprise College, Nuneaton

URSULA'S FLASHBACK

There I was, sitting in the palace, on the throne, Sebastian by my side, when Neptune barged in, stole my trident and wiped everyone's memories but mine. He forced me off my chair.

I called out, "Guards!" but no one came. I screamed again, "Guards!"

But Neptune rudely said, "You're no longer queen, Ursula. I am the ruler now."

I asked, "Why? Why are you doing this?"

He replied, "Life's full of tough choices, isn't it?" Then, from the top of his lungs, he screamed, "Guards!"

They took me away as I shouted, "Now I plot my revenge!" He scoffed.

Summer Wynn-Blackburn (13)
Holbrook Academy, Holbrook

LOKI

Suddenly, the door to the cells bursts open as Thor thunders in and rapidly begins searching the cells, looking for the one worth anything to him: mine.

"We need to talk!" booms Thor.

"Can't you see I'm busy?" I smirk.

"Enough of your games brother. Where is it?" he demands, anger in his eyes.

"What are you on about? Honestly, you're losing it." I retort, getting annoyed. Looking astonished and puzzled, I take a breather and slowly stride forward. Looking Thor in the eyes, I say (albeit unconvincingly), "I don't know what you're on about."

Thor smashes the bars.

Aliesha Ranson
Holbrook Academy, Holbrook

CERBERUS

I'm nothing but a guard dog to the underworld. I'm loyal and kind, yet I'm viewed like I'm some sort of teras.
I have three gigantic heads, which definitely makes me less appealing to people who read my story. Yet if they looked deeper into the story, they'd know how tormented I really am.
Hades, he looks after me. Really the only god I see. I see mortal souls being brought down by Psyche, they always look so distressed and petrified. It almost makes me wonder why I'm stuck to these chains, forced to watch them for all eternity.

Amelia Bloomfiled (15)
Holbrook Academy, Holbrook

WILLIAM THE WICKED WIZARD

I stood, stirring my potion to hopefully demolish my arch-nemesis, George the Great. Until I heard a crashing noise upstairs. Hurrying to make sure nobody, even my partner in crime, could see what I was creating.

However, when I arrived at the room where the noise had come from, nobody was there. So I strolled back down to my cauldron. However, as I got back, George the Great was standing there, looking at my potion, trying to figure out what the substance was.

But before he knew it, I pushed him into the scorching cauldron.

James Pook (13)
Holbrook Academy, Holbrook

MEDUSA

Is this the end? My final breath is to be cast in this cave, which I have been restricted to, all because of him. That stupid God of the Oceans, Poseidon. He is the reason for my downfall, for my pain and suffering.

I was beautiful. The entitled God took it upon himself to have me as his own. Then that selfish man was so careless to let his affair be seen by Athena.

Oh, how she ruined me. Turning me into such a hideous creature, I had to flee from Olympia. And now, I'm to be slain... damned Poseidon.

Miles Marazzi (16)
Holbrook Academy, Holbrook

KING OF ASGARD

As I watch Thor walk down the palace to Father, I'm furious at Father for choosing Thor over me. I'm the rightful king, it should be me. As I storm out, Mother calls for me, shouting my name, telling me to stop.

I walk to the treasure room and see the Tesseract in all its might. As I go up and grab it, I see my hands turn blue. I turn into a frost giant!

I grab the Tesseract and walk up, quietly, to my brother's chambers. I stand in my glory and boom, "The King of Asgard is gone."

Lilly-Mai King (14)
Holbrook Academy, Holbrook

QUEEN OF HEARTS

I was sitting on my throne, getting ready for the party in honour of my mother who had recently died. Everything was going perfectly. The roses were white, the tablecloth was white, and the guards were where Mother always placed them. Then I heard screams coming from the garden!
I rushed out to see what the panic was about. There I saw the roses painted! Red on the tablecloths and the guards dead!
I looked at who was the culprit. A blonde girl in a blue dress and a white apron. Off with her head now, I say!

Molly Alice Wainwright (14)
Holbrook Academy, Holbrook

THE WITCH WITH DARK MAGIC

A witch was always hiding from good. She had dark magic. She tried spell after spell after spell and she had finally got it: the curse for the good to have badness inside them. But she missed out on the younger generation. But she already had a plan to get them. She was going to capture them and make them her children and make them evil. Could they escape before the time ran out? Could they escape? The witch had hunted them down where they were and could curse them.

Lillie Howlett (11)
Holbrook Academy, Holbrook

MEETING MISSY HOOK

I've been banished to Earth. Humans may have heard of fallen angels but not fallen Achamelon. So, when a girl human, Missy Hook, befriended me and took me to her home, I had some teaching to do.

She lived in a floating house in a place called Harbour. We spent hours trying to pronounce our names.

"Achmamleone?" she tried.

"No. Ach-am-el-on," I'd correct. And correct. Until.

"Achamelon!" Missy danced up and down, and I joined her. It was the first time I'd felt joy, but it stopped abruptly.

Clang! Scrape! The door opened and a shining metal point peeped in.

Erin May Jarratt (11)
Holmleigh Park High School, Tuffley

APOCALYPSE'S DYING WORDS

I thought I belonged, but I'm now more alone than ever. This taste of acid, taste of defeat, is choking me. What happened? What happened to that child who wanted to morph the world? And I was good, too.

I'm so full of fear now. There's not a sliver of hope in this world. My days in the universe are done. Soon that wretched arrow, the thing that has brought me so much confusion, will soon be in my empty heart.

"I wanted to fight," I say, "for a country of peace. Well, goodbye. You are all better without me."

Eloise Medd (12)
Holmleigh Park High School, Tuffley

LAST BREATH

He lay there, watching the sunset as life slipped from his body. I stalked across the rubbled land toward him, then pulled down my sable hood. He was young and smiled weakly up at me. Three words drifted from his lips, "Is it time?" They echoed. They always echoed.

I nodded. He gazed upon the world a final time. Then he closed his eyes. I gathered him in my arms, gently, carefully. A tree's branches wavered as the last rays of sunlight brushed a quivering leaf. Then darkness, my darkness, flooded everything.

Jac Griffiths
Holmleigh Park High School, Tuffley

OBEY HER

Bellatrix Lestrange was an independent individual. Her crimes would never be forgotten. But was Bellatrix always how she'd been in the later stages of her life? Or was there a whole unexplored side of her?

Young Bellatrix bounced down the stairs with a bright smile on her face, before seeing her 'dear' mother and father's stern expression on their faces. She stopped at once.

She had always been told that she was an accident and they wanted a boy. These words impacted her and, sometimes, she even struggled to imagine her own parents would say that to her.

Leonie Trinh (11)
Holyport College, Holyport

A FORGOTTEN PROMISE

I haven't forgotten...

"Michael! This is not who you are! Snap out of it! Please!"

Not all stories have a beginning like this one. You may think it's a happy story that always ends with a happy ending. No. This story is a story I'll never forget. An unfortunate memory.

"Please don't. Please... You promised..."

Something I'll regret for the rest of my life. From that day on, my life changed forever. Leaving a promise to myself for a brighter future. But years pass and that future just seems like a past dream that has become a forgotten promise.

Hela Nikben (14)
Madani Girls' School, Whitechapel

TENTACLES

Ursula watched the little mermaid come in with a bittersweetness, from the shadows of her cave. This was a girl who was accepted in a kingdom of mer, who had a family, and who was a precious treasure to King Triton. Triton, who'd exiled her when she was just a young witch, orphaned with nowhere to go, and with a desire to start her new life in the kingdom. She wasn't accepted, due to her differences from her people.

Instead of being welcomed, she was banished, nearly arrested by King Triton's wrath. Triton thought of her as harm, an evil.

Caitlin Pujol (17)
Poplar Adolescent Unit, Rochford

IMMORTALITY

It was done to survive. Venom submerged my every breath.
One hour 'til they perish, one hour 'til their demise.
All my life I was enclosed. It felt like I was on the path of life
or death. My time was not the same, not here. I rotted here
for decades. I have committed what some wouldn't dare
attempt. I would have turned insane years ago, if it wasn't
for Paris.
Only some know the meaning of life, but few go beyond, few
break the barrier of immortality.

Harrison Baxter
Purbrook Park School, Purbrook

DO I DESERVE HAPPINESS?

Do I deserve happiness? A thought replaying in my head, consuming my emotions, the way I think. My powers felt like a burden, attracting bad luck. 'Til I fell in love with her. She understood me. Took one glance and instantly acknowledged the pain residing in me. For a time, that pain disappeared and was replaced by a cluster of joy. But everything must come to an end. Even things close to my heart.

As they found me, those monsters! Took everything, my wife, my child, my heart. People who call themselves just, made me a villain. Made me Magneto.

Talha Ajaz (16)
Solihull Sixth Form College, Solihull

LIGHT OR FLIGHT

I fumble around in the cupboard and shake anxiety pills onto my hand. The curtains stay closed. On the counter, there is a glass filled up with something that resembles cranberry juice.

When eating leftover spaghetti, I burn my tongue and blood starts to settle onto my fangs. I think back to when I first started the famous rumour that vampires perish in sunlight. We are all just dysfunctional and socially awkward.

I got my name from the time I stubbed my toe on a sofa. In that moment, I called out 'Dracula'.

Aishah Begum (16)
Solihull Sixth Form College, Solihull

THE STORY OF CHAVE

One stormy night, Chave had a bad nightmare that he was facing the evil Chicken God. Chave's powers were his ability to shoot lasers out of his eyes.

In his dream, Chave felt like he had lightning going through his body.

As lightning flashed through the sky, Chave saw the Chicken God! Chave rushed out of bed and went to end it once and for all. They both began to fight but Chave's powers didn't work.

The Chicken God had a cursed carrot which killed Chave as he got too near. Rest in peace, Chave.

Stan Seaman
Springboard Education, Lancing

WHAT IF BLACK MANTA WON?

"Finally, my plan succeeded!" Black Manta laughed manically, looking at Aquaman's lifeless body. "I can rule the seas with Aquaman's trident!"

Firstly, Black Manta caused mayhem by building a giant castle, crushing many homes. Next, he made everyone obey his rules and bring him treasure. To increase his vast fortune, he used his control of the seas to sell fish species into extinction.

Humanity would be forever terrified to approach the water. The oxygen would fall because of reduced ocean plants. Due to Black Manta's changes, the oceans became a barren wasteland, like a watery hell.

Alfie Morrow (11)
St Killian's College, Carnlough

ONCE UPON A NIGHTMARE

Up in the castle lay a beautiful princess known as Aurora. Time was ticking but still no sign of the Prince. She only had until midnight for the curse to be broken. If the curse wasn't broken, she would never see daylight again.

Finally, the Prince arrived, just in time. He went to kiss her, but nothing happened. He then realised it was too late to save his love. Too late to save the one he cared about the most.

He saw a window and bolted out to see what could end this nightmare - except this one was real.

Maggie Steele (12)

St Killian's College, Carnlough

FROZEN WAS ALL A LIE

Anna was finally victorious. She had won. Let me tell you how it all started.

Years ago, a mysterious figure ran up to Elsa and gave her powers. She was never born with them. This figure could tell the future and knew that Anna would try to get rid of Elsa. Anna never forgot that Elsa had hurt her so long ago.

Elsa couldn't hurt Anna because she cared and loved her so much, so she made the ice castle to run away from Anna so she couldn't hurt her. She knew what would happen next. Anna had won.

Abigail Morrow (11)

St Killian's College, Carnlough

WORDS CAUSED THE BEAST

Oh, I can't explain it, my emotions are too strong.
One mean comment and my happiness is gone!
Oh, I can't explain it, if I did I'd go insane.
I'd walk into school and they would say, "Imagine being him!
What a loser!" They'd whisper it or scream it, and once that
happened... an insane monster I became.
So insane, I'd feast for blood or flesh.
So insane, I'd break a window or chair.
So insane, I'd take a bite out of my teacher!
Oh no, I'd done it. Hello, please do come closer... so I can
eat you.

Naoise Murphy (12)
St Louise's Comprehensive College, Belfast

HEARTBROKEN

Love. Find love, feel love. That's all I was taught to do. When I finally found it, I got hurt. Hi, I'm Heartbroken.
You're probably wondering why I sound so depressed about love. That's because I found out what it actually feels like. Yes, it feels great when you're in it, but as soon as you get hurt by it, it feels like you can't breathe, you're drowning. Everyone said I would forget about it, eventually. But people forget that love can be a dangerous thing. So the question is: is love evil or can I just not find it?

Jamey Holland (13)
St Louise's Comprehensive College, Belfast

THE STORY OF HADES

I wasn't always evil, I haven't always been feared. I'm Hades, ruler of the Underworld, and this is my story.
I was with two of my brothers, Zeus and Poseidon. They were acting strangely, but I assumed it was because we hadn't chosen someone to rule the Underworld.
Then they spoke. "Hades, could we speak with you?" they asked.
I followed them to a room, where they zapped me. I tried to fight back but they were too strong. I woke up in a dark place. I guess they chose someone to rule the Underworld...

Nikita Carlin
St Louise's Comprehensive College, Belfast

THE GOAT MAN

Kevin Lawlor was on the run from the police because he was an escaped convict and a serial killer. He was shot in the back, dropped to the ground, and bled out.

Five fiery arms came out of the ground and pulled his corpse to Hell. He arrived there and saw the fiery pit and heard the blood-curdling screams from the others around him.

He saw a goat-like creature standing before him and, with his deep voice, he said, "You're too evil, even for here." Kevin was banished, doomed to roam the earth as the Goat Man.

Jackson O'Riordan (12)
St Louise's Comprehensive College, Belfast

CANCER

I did it to survive. I'd come too far to stop now. All those years of growing were too much, and I was not going to let the humans stop me.

Yes, I felt guilty taking all of those lives, but they fuelled me and drove me crazy. My family needed the souls to thrive on, and we could not afford another survivor, for we would shrink, like a candle burning out.

They would not beat me. They would not beat Cancer.

Eve Rose Maguire (13)

St Louise's Comprehensive College, Belfast

DONNIE DARKO

I thought I was going crazy, seeing the bunny every day, everywhere, every time. When I looked in the mirror, I started to believe I was turning into him. I felt like I had to be him to save someone else. Was I turning into him? Was I him, but just a human version? I found it hard to decide if I wanted to be him or not. I had a family and friends, but if he was me, he wouldn't care what I did or thought...

Lana Sutcliffe (13)
St Louise's Comprehensive College, Belfast

SHERE KHAN

Once a boy, now a tiger. Revenge was now a certainty. "I will never forgive you, Mowgli! Never!"
Lungri was having a fun day with his brother, Mowgli, until something went terribly wrong. Lungri had a strange feeling, as if he was suddenly unwell.
"I need some sleep," he said. However, when he woke up, he was faced with doom!
The eleven-year-old boy was now furry, thin, and had paws! He was a tiger! He tried to get out of bed, his brothers screamed. He was startled, so he ran. And so his revenge began...

Lucy Wood (12)
St Mark's West Essex Catholic School, Harlow

THE CUBE QUEEN

After operation Sky Fire, the whole island was covered in cubes and the Cube Queen had awakened. Why did she do it? On the Cube Queen's own planet, Cubism, she had a brother who was voted to be King - even though she was meant to be Queen.

This was Slone's fault because Slone persuaded the Cube Queen's brother into stealing the throne. She tried to become Queen but she was then cast off her own planet. After, she settled on a planet called Reality 0 where she started to build her empire - to take revenge on Slone!

Finley Sweeting (11)
St Mark's West Essex Catholic School, Harlow

THE END OF THE ROAD

A waterfall of grief haunts me as I fade away into blackness. The man was still reasonably young but he welcomed me with open arms. I cradled him gently as his family screamed and sobbed in pain. He sighed as they drifted slowly into a hazy mist, and then lay still.

Why do they hate me? I don't understand. My job is to help them in their final hours, to ease the pain and suffering of both them and their family. Grief is hard but some are glad to see me. Remember, I open a new door in their lives.

Maisie Preston (12)

St Michael's CE High School, Chorley

THE SCARS YOU LEFT BEHIND

My plan was perfectly brewed. "Get them ready, Janari." She scurried into the bushes. With that dealt with, I watched as Thale embraced the applause of the civilians. My body boiled, I had to make an entrance.

"Miss me, Thale?"

"What brings you here, outcast?"

"Outcast? Wasn't it *you* who shot the President, bombed the House of Ministers? Yet *I'm* the outcast?" The civilians looked at Thale, shocked. Just as planned.

"There's no proof!"

"Isn't there?" I grinned as Janari arrived with the army. Thale stared, his eyes dilated in terror.

"You won the battle, but I'll win the war..."

Kosi Onwuneme (12)
St Robert Of Newminster, Fatfield

TEMPTED TOO FAR

Forced into a corner. One billion pounds, you'd be tempted too. My family needed the money. What choice was there? So, I followed the plan.

Bombs in place, trigger in my hand. My hands lingered above the switch. The fate of the world in my hands. *Click! Click! Click!* Broken, useless, destroyed.

Suddenly, the door burst open. Heavily armed men circled around me. "Get down on the floor, hands in the air!" The sentence that broke me, changed my life forever.

My mind stilled as my body, motionless, as they wrestled me to the ground. Locked up for all eternity.

Sam Green (12)
St Robert Of Newminster, Fatfield

ETERNAL REVENGE

The heat is overwhelming. The fire is biting at my flesh. How long until these ropes burn out? Will the audience leave before the fire goes out and I'm free? They can't find out my secret, that I'm immortal.

Us witches don't deserve this, we aren't the monsters that mankind think we are, but then again, they really are gullible. I tricked them, the mere mortals really think I'm burning at the stake. Illusion spells really aren't that hard when you're from a coven of witches.

I watch as they celebrate my death, but soon I will be celebrating theirs.

Lucy Lodge (13)
St Robert Of Newminster, Fatfield

PAST

There are many monsters in this world. Many hide in the dark, many you see every day. There is one monster I saw every time, through mirrors.

"Mummy, why does everyone hate death?" I was a child when I asked my mother this question. Mother told me that life created us and death was a killer. The only cruel person was my mother, who created me as a monster.

"Sweetie, we are going to be late." The last time I held my mum's soft hand. "Children are so disgusting, take him away!"

Mothers are supposed be guardian angels, right? "Mum!"

Neyatha Vinoy
St Robert Of Newminster, Fatfield

MY REVENGE

I was finally here, the place where my father was kidnapped. I went inside the prison and saw people working. But then I saw him.

I ran to him and told him I had come to save him, but he refused to leave. He told me that he was an important person in this prison and everybody obeyed him. I got very angry with him and had no other choice but to kill him.

So my conquest began, I freed village after village from all of these peacemakers who brought evil. And so people were under my control.

Ronnie Chan (13)
St Robert Of Newminster, Fatfield

A HEAD

The head sits on the mahogany table, neck skin torn so prettily, the material flaps about the still-spilling opening. It's facing straight, concentrating, as if still facing the opponent.
The viewer can be assured that it was found, if they so virtuously worry about the conditions in which the body met its' ends with the head. The sentimental mind would have wanted the entire soldier. The mud it was forgotten in too. But the goal is to paint a work that will shock those fools and fill my bank with it.
I must make haste before the blood dries.

Tilly Milner (14)
St Thomas More RC Academy, North Shields

THE REVENGE OF HE WHO CANNOT BE NAMED

It's Voldemort here. I killed Lily and James for a reason. Harry is my son. My dear boy who disappeared eleven years ago. I've been searching for him and his kidnappers ever since.

Once I found them, I begged them for him back but they disagreed. So I gave them what they deserved: death. They took my one and only, so I took their one and only life.

My whole life has been hunting and hiding since that stormy night when my life changed. I'm writing this in hiding, hoping that someone will find it. I'm dying. I need help.

Evie Race (11)

St Thomas More RC Academy, North Shields

A STONE-COLD VIEW

Banished because no one could bear to look at me. Accompanied by only the snakes on my head. All because he violated me. Why did she punish me? Day and night their names run through my head. Poseidon. Athena. Poseidon. Athena. It's all because of them. I'm here because of them.

Looking in my eyes, men turned to stone. I hated it, then I realised they wanted my head as a trophy. Their king wanted to gift it to her! Athena! Athena! Athena! One after another, men came and stayed. Because so long as I can't leave, neither can they...

Gracie Davis (15)
St Thomas More RC Academy, North Shields

THINGS AREN'T ALWAYS WHAT THEY SEEM

My fingers scraped the edge of the silver keychain. So close. A little further and I'd have them. The freezing rain lashed against my face as the wind whipped my hair.

I saw a figure! He was racing towards me. Fast! I was frozen to the spot like a Greek statue caught by Medusa's stare. I felt helpless as his huge tattooed arms clamped around me like a vice and we fell.

Smash! The scaffolding crashed into the exact spot where I was standing. I jumped up! I was alone. I opened my fist and there were my keys.

Sophia Dodds (11)

St Thomas More RC Academy, North Shields

TWISTED

Blood dripped down through the cracks from the floorboards above. I continued to chew emotionlessly. My grey eyes stared out into the grim street.

In the distance, through a window, I could see another depressed family. The mother a drunk, the father a drug addict. They hadn't seen their daughter for two weeks. I laughed hysterically before stopping to continue watching. Their marriage had been in shambles even before their daughter disappeared. She started screaming again which brought me round to my senses. I grumbled and limped up the stairs, my leg crying with pain. Their daughter was too noisy.

Thomas Baars
St Thomas The Apostle College, Nunhead

WHAT REALLY HAPPENS IN THE GINGERBREAD HOUSE

I still haven't forgotten the first child's scream, her horrified face and the pang of guilt. After a while it got easier, the guilt slowly fading away.

I licked my fingers clean of blood, sat down on my creaking wooden rocking chair, and waited for the sweet sound of children. You must be wondering why I do this. Well, it's simple really, it makes me younger. It takes years worth of wrinkles off my face.

I hear them! Children! Ooh, it sounds like two. Smells like bony ones. Ahh, that's okay, I can fatten them up. Here they come. "Hello?"

Eva Richards (13)
Stirling High School, Stirling

WHO LOVES THE VILLAIN?

Everyone loves heroes, like Batman and Iron Man. But no one loves the villain. They're always perceived as this cold-hearted person who could never love.

Well, in my case, that's accurate. Anyway, backstory over, time to jump back into reality.

I walk away from the exploding building. Proud of myself for what I've achieved. With the money I have just taken, I run to pay my dad's hospital bills. Once I've finished with that, I have some good guys to kill. I crack my knuckles and get started. It's for a good cause after all...

Izzy W
Stockport School, Stockport

THE LAST TIME

I didn't mean to. I didn't *want* to hurt the Robinsons'. But I did. It was Sunday, me and Jeremy had a feud. A feud with guns, actually.

I was amazed by the defence moves he'd learnt, but soon worried to see that I wasn't getting anything out of it. The gun was fiddly in my hands and was aimed at his head. At first, I was teasing him, but then the revolver went off. He was dead. I was laughing right after.

"Stop acting." I turned round to hear a beep, somebody had caught it all on camera.

Adiba Rahman (11)
Swanlea School, Whitechapel

THE PYROMANIAC

I did it to be loved. I did it to be noticed. I ended thousands of lives for my sake. Finally, my time had come, my time to be the villain of the century. No one loved me as a child and now I'd have no mercy!

Burning fumes entered my nose and my face lit up with a grin. The sound of people suffering made me laugh. Now people would know how I'd felt as a child.

Burning building after building and destroying city after city, I screamed, "How does it feel to be in pain? This is fun!"

Ruqayyah Chowdhury
Swanlea School, Whitechapel

THE PSYCHOPATH

As a child, nobody understood me. It was like everyone was envious of me. I had no friends at all, but I never understood why.

I killed the hero and here's why: he lied about who he was. It was a lie! I saw he had kidnapped billions of people. I did what I had to. Maybe the kidnapped people would tell, but they stayed quiet. Nobody believed me.

I was about to be killed, so I killed everyone who hated me. Nobody was left in the village. I felt lonely but happy. I got the taste for revenge.

Afreen Khan (12)
Swanlea School, Whitechapel

GRIM REAPER

"Dad, I thought you said all the greatest villains only ever have to win once?"

"I was right then and I still am."

"Then how come you're the greatest villain of all time and you've won countless times?"

"Don't pull a face like that. Not even I win every time, or on the first try, but the most patient villains are the ones who win. There's no need to hurry, they'll come knocking at Death's door themselves when they're ready. Now, quick, before another poor soul knocks on the door, I'd like to have some tea."

Ruth Ogbuokiri (13)

Sydney Russell School, Dagenham

ONLY IN YOUR NIGHTMARES

It's me! I did all of it. But how would the stupid humans find out? Through my vicious red eyes, only I know the truth! They don't worry about the data of the deaths increasing. They don't even suspect any harm from me.

I'm the quiet neighbour no one notices. No one ever thinks that I do anything but sit in the dark of my house. They're all wrong! Whatever they predict, it'll never be close to who I am today.

I am the animal who leaves scraps of blood everywhere. I am the one who drains everyone to death.

Elisa Gjoka (13)

Sydney Russell School, Dagenham

MY BELLY RUMBLED

From the middle of the forest I could smell the juiciest meat ahead of me. I had to take my chances! I ran, untamed, toward the window.

I was lucky, she was sleeping. I inched toward her, then gobbled her up whole. Immediately, I heard footsteps. There was no time, I had to pretend to be her. I lay in her bed and waited.

"Oh, Grandma, what big teeth you have!"

I had to think quickly. I whispered, "I have them to smile at you, dear." She would be next! I would enjoy her, slowly. My belly rumbled again...

Kevin Gjoka (12)
Sydney Russell School, Dagenham

THE GINGERBREAD MAN

Toasting nicely... "Oh no!"

"We left the gingerbread men in the oven!"

"Uh-oh, we can't sell these, they're burnt," said the baker to his wife. "I'll leave them out to cool, then we can practise icing on them."

Thirty minutes later, the baker and his wife picked up the burnt gingerbread men and started to ice one.

First the trousers, then the dots to stick the buttons on, then finally his eyes and mouth. To the couple's surprise, the gingerbread man jumped off the tray and yelled, "You burned me, now I'll eat you!"

The gingerbread man started chasing them.

Freddie Clarke (11)

The Costello School, Basingstoke

CINDERELLA

Cinderella's stepmother was extremely annoyed at Cinderella because the Prince loved her, not her daughters. She decided to trap her in a small, mysterious room with no way out.

It'd been days and days since Cinderella had been trapped, but then something awful happened. The stepmother decided to poison Cinderella while she was eating.

The stepmother put the poison in her food the next morning, so her daughters could be royal, famous and wealthy. A few months later, everyone found out what the stepmother did and she was immediately arrested for what she had done to Cinderella that fateful day.

Jasmina Mackowiak (12)
The Costello School, Basingstoke

CINDERELLA

Lily was Cinderella's sister. She wasn't as happy as you might've thought. Mother never paid much attention to Lily, unlike Lola, her twin. Lola got a bag filled with presents for her birthday. Unsurprisingly, Lily didn't get any. Instead, she was blamed for her sister's failed school report.

Once the prince came, Lola was desperate for his money, Lily just wanted to be free. Cinderella and Lily had an amazing relationship in secret, best friends forever. When the prince took Cinderella, Lily was heartbroken. To this day, Lily is 53 but still held hostage by the evil Lola.

Natasza Wijata (11)
The Costello School, Basingstoke

CINDERELLA

Cinderella was married to the prince. However, what you've been told was not the whole truth.

The sisters should have earned the place, not Cindy. She was the one who murdered her own mother - it wasn't an accident. She deserved to get two stepsisters, it was her fault for killing her mother. She cheated her way to victory by using magic.

However, her stepmother and stepsisters took hard work and time to impress the prince. Only to find Ella stealing their happiness. How cruel. How would you like it if an evil stepsibling took your hard work by cheating?

Meggy Meng (12)
The Costello School, Basingstoke

POPPY AND PEARL

Once upon a time, there were twins called Poppy and Pearl. They were relaxing on the beach when Pearl had the idea to go looking for treasure. Poppy agreed and both started searching.

"Oh, let's put shells down so we don't get lost," said Poppy. Pearl gave a slight nod and kept on walking. They continued walking until they had a small bucket of beach treasures. However, when they looked back, the tide had taken all the shells away. Oh no!

Suddenly, as they turned around to walk back, a cloaked figure grabbed both of the twins and they disappeared!

Amaya O'Sullivan (11)

The Costello School, Basingstoke

THE THREE PIGS

The evil piggies came to the last wolf. "Hey, little wolf, let us come in."

"No! Not by the hairs on my chinny chin chin!"

"Then I'll snort and I'll snort and I'll snort your house down." And so, the piggies did.

The last wolf rang Little Red Riding Hood to come and save him. Seconds, well, realistically, minutes later, there was Red Riding Hood! She pulled her gun out of her knickers and shot the evil pigs dead.

Then she killed the last wolf and used its skin as a lovely new wolfskin cloak. Then off she skipped.

Stan Trussler (11)

The Costello School, Basingstoke

SMALL PEOPLE, BIG THINGS

It. Didn't. Work. I still haven't forgotten the way those little freaks destroyed my plan. I was after the ability she had and they failed me. That 'special' little girl.

We lured her in with luscious-smelling roses and a cutesy little cottage. We let her die. I was going to use my powers to extract her ability. The ability I wanted. The ability to talk to animals. The creatures of the woods would be my slaves. Then we dwarfs would reign supreme.

But, I'll succeed. I will get you back, Snow White. Watch your back. Dopey will find you.

Jess Croxon (11)
The Costello School, Basingstoke

THREE LITTLE PIGS

Once upon a time, there were three little pigs and a wolf. The wolf was hungry and wanted some roast pig.

The pigs started to make homes, one straw, one wood and one brick. The three pigs saw the wolf coming. One created a distraction, while the others sprinted to the brick house where they were safe!

The brick pig was prepared and when the wolf came, he shouted, "Ah, some lovely roasted wolf!"

The wolf yelped, "What makes you think you can beat me?"

The pig got out a shotgun and shot the wolf! "We get supper after all!"

Josh Somerville (12)
The Costello School, Basingstoke

THREE BILLY GOATS GRUFF

Darren, Stan, and Rippley were eating some grass when they found three unusual mushrooms. They ate them and discovered they were in a palace, which was a bit like a maze. They realised they were no longer goats, they were superheroes!

Darren was a ninja, Stan was a wizard and Rippley was a strong guy with a spiky club. They separated, going different ways. On the way, they found lots of monsters. Using their powers, they defeated everyone and came close to the exit, meeting each other.

Then there was a huge monster! Rippley killed him with one shot.

Rakshit Saravanakumar (11)
The Costello School, Basingstoke

THE HEARTLESS GHOST

On a dark, desolate night, all was silent besides the moaning and crying of the ghost. His wisp of tears fell onto the ground and evaporated into the mourning night. His cries grew stronger; he was searching for his lost love who wept in despair, in the human world.

All the cries grew louder and more sorrowful. Then, *crunch*... A human girl found the source of the flat moans. The human called the village witch and she created a spell to suck all love and happiness out of the forlorn ghost.

He never found his lost love; he stopped looking.

Ana Patel-Potter (11)
The Costello School, Basingstoke

SNOW WHITE

I still haven't forgotten the promise I made to my mother; to be the queen of beauty. The most beautiful. I wanted to continue her beauty and let her spirit live on, so she'd be proud.

Now I have to complete with this person named Snow White that my magic mirror described. All these years of work, just to be beaten by some wandering maid. I can just imagine what my mother would say: "You're pathetic."

I have to stop her from winning this fight. I will not let my legacy of beauty be destroyed. I promise, Mother, I'll win.

Max Huang (11)
The Costello School, Basingstoke

LITTLE RED RIDING HOOD

Once upon a time, Little Red Riding Hood went on a walk to find something to eat. Later on that day, Little Red Riding Hood found a house. She knocked on the door and asked, "Can I come in? I'm cold."

The nan said, "Yes, sweetie, come in."

Little Red Riding Hood said, "Oh, thank you so much!"

Nan said, "Do you want a drink and something to eat?"

The girl shook her head, gobbled the nan up and put her clothes on to wait for the wolf to arrive. When the wolf arrived, Little Red Riding Hood shot him.

Leon Hynan (12)
The Costello School, Basingstoke

THE THREE LITTLE WOLVES

Not long ago, there were three little wolves. They lived happily with their mother. Well, not for very long. They didn't know that their mother thought it would be best if they moved out. So they did.

They started a new life among the woods. The three wolves made amazing houses. Just as they got cosy, there was a knock on the door. Three horrible little pigs called Porky, Chop, and Sausages charged at the innocent wolves.

The three wolves screamed in horror as the pigs decided to gobble the wolves up and lived horribly ever after.

Charleigh Connoley (11)
The Costello School, Basingstoke

HANSEL AND GRETEL

Once upon an evil day, in a small town, lived the evil children, Hansel and Gretel. They were kicked out of their home and forced to live in the woods.

The next day, they found a gingerbread house full of sweets. Hansel and Gretel decided to eat the sweets. Then an old witch came out of the house.

She trapped Hansel and Gretel. She tried putting Hansel in the oven, the children pushed her in and ate her whole. They went back to their old house, planning to eat their parents. They gobbled them up, but Hansel was still hungry...

Holly Wolldridge (11)
The Costello School, Basingstoke

THREE LITTLE PIGS

Once upon a time, there were three little pigs. One pig built its house out of straw, the second pig built its house out of sticks, the third pig built its house of bricks.

One day, the three little pigs were in their houses, until Little Red Riding Hood managed to capture them. She took them to the wolf!

When they were there, there were many other animals that Little Red Riding Hood had caught for the wolf. The wolf decided he wanted to eat the three little pigs.

They all shouted, "You're never going to eat us!" and ran.

James Ennis (12)
The Costello School, Basingstoke

DIE, MY BEAUTY!

I was so close. So close! I've got a better plan this time. The prince. He'll be mine! He kisses her and she wakes up! Done! The same plan, just not only one of them! I'll act when he's sleeping, so I'll find him now!
My magic will do the trick just fine, so, Prince, say bye-bye! His red blood spilling on the floor, so Princey is no more! Aurora, prick your fingers, so I won't have to linger!
Now my plan's gone through and through, I'll do what the evil queen couldn't do! Say goodbye to Snow White!

Immy Kane (11)
The Costello School, Basingstoke

SCAR'S REDEMPTION

I had to make up for what I'd done. My greed and jealousy had ruined Pride Rock. I regretted ruining Simba's life and realised that he should have been king. I regretted killing Mufasa and dooming Pride Rock to fall to the neighbouring hyenas. I regretted...

Enough regret. I had to make up for my actions. My mind was made up and I would leave tomorrow. I hadn't been back to Pride Rock since the attack. I wondered how much things had changed. At dawn tomorrow, I would set off. I would make Pride Rock forgive me. I knew it.

Charlie McLoughlin (12)
The Costello School, Basingstoke

THE PRINCESS AND THE PIN

Once upon a time, there was a princess who never really belonged. She went out on adventures without permission. While she was on an adventure to a run-down castle, she saw a handsome prince who was also exploring the castle. She decided to go closer to him. It was love at first sight! They spoke for hours, she took him to her castle. Unfortunately, the king was full of hate. In the prince's bed, he put a needle that expanded when pressure was put on it. When the prince slept on the needle, it pierced his heart. He dropped dead!

Saira Shrestha (11)
The Costello School, Basingstoke

LITTLE RED RIDING HOOD

Once upon a time, there was a girl called Little Red Riding Hood. She lived in a place called Las Vegas and she was a gangster (someone who steals things and kills people). However, the wolf was a good guy and protected the city from Little Red Riding Hood and other gangsters.

Little Red Riding Hood walked into the biggest museum in the world and stole all the best things. The security guards called the wolf and the wolf found her and took the stolen items back. He put her in jail for life. Everyone else lived happily ever after.

Ethan Spurway (12)

The Costello School, Basingstoke

THREE HUNGRY WOLVES

There were three hungry wolves. They decided to go hunting out in the woods. The smallest wolf stumbled across a house made of bricks. As he looked through the window, the wolf saw a massive pig, who'd last him for a whole week. The wolf kept this a secret.

As he knocked on the door, he could hear the pig walking to the door. Now, you may think this wolf would be sly, smart and fast. Unfortunately, you're thinking the exact opposite. When he was ready to attack, the pig saw him and ate him up in one big gobble.

Kashish Ghale (11)
The Costello School, Basingstoke

SNOW WHITE AND THE SEVEN DWARFS

Once upon a time, there was a very smart and beautiful girl, her name was Snow White. As she was so beautiful, her stepsisters envied her and her stepmother hated her because she got more attention than her sisters. So Snow White was locked up.

One day, seven dwarfs went on an adventure and they saw Snow White crying in her room. The dwarfs decided to knock on the front door. They were greeted by the mother. Cleverly, they pretended to be sick and were brought up to a guest room. They then hatched a plan to rescue Snow White.

Nicole Villavicencio Duran (11)

The Costello School, Basingstoke

THE OGRE

Once upon a time, there was an ogre who was called Shrek. He was walking down through the forest, then he tripped on a twig.

He woke up in a magical land of leaves. He explored it and found a donkey who fell for the trap too. The donkey's name was Bob and he helped Shrek from then on.

They explored the land more and found three little pigs and a big bad wolf. They all became friends until the big bad wolf betrayed them, eating the three little pigs. "You're next, donkey," said the wolf in a scary voice.

Alex West (11)
The Costello School, Basingstoke

THE BOY IN THE VAN

A boy was walking late at night. He stopped, suddenly seeing a van driving down the usually quiet road next to him. He started running, thinking it was a kidnapper. The van sped up to him and someone pulled him inside the back of the van.

A large bag got pulled over his head and someone was holding him still. He was sweating, crying, and screaming all at once.

The van stopped all of a sudden. He heard footsteps trotting around the van. The back door opened and his uncle Connor appeared. The boy was shocked and surprised!

Olly Tavendale (11)

The Costello School, Basingstoke

BILLY GOATS GRUFF

I still haven't forgotten the time when I had a curse put on me. I claimed a bridge as 'mine' and didn't let anyone go through it.

It all started when I met this lady and she offered me an apple. I said yes and then, unbelievably, I got cursed. Three billy goats came to 'my' bridge and tried to get through. I wouldn't let them. Then it hit me. I realised I was cursed and fought back.

It worked! I apologised and let the goats through. I hope they know I'm not a bad person and I was cursed.

Magi Kasabova (11)
The Costello School, Basingstoke

THREE SILLY SHEEP

Once upon a time, there lived three silly sheep. One day, Sammy, Sally and Suzy went on a walk over a bridge. Then a friendly troll came out of nowhere.

All three sheep said to the troll, "We want to fight you."

But, Tina, the troll said, "No, I want to fight you."

Sammy was not going without a fight, so Sammy went up to the troll and started to kick her. Tina the troll got angry so she picked up Sally and ate her. Then Sally kicked, so Tina ate Sally. Suzy then kicked Tina and got eaten too!

Brooke Olive (11)
The Costello School, Basingstoke

THE ALIEN BOY

There once was a boy called Bob and everyone would say that he was an alien because he only had one eye. Bob was adopted but he didn't know. One day, he got so fed up of all the bullies that he ran home and cried.

His mum heard him crying, so she went into his room. She asked him if he was okay and he said, "Yes, I'm fine."

His mum asked him, "Are you sure?"

That's when he started crying again, and said what was really happening. His mum felt really bad and she was very worried.

Ameliah Ward (11)
The Costello School, Basingstoke

THE THREE PIGS

I was hiding behind a tree when I saw them. The pigs. I was looking for the house with the three pigs.

There I was, blowing the house down. It was only made of straw. In a huff and a puff, the house was down. The pigs started crying and I felt bad.

After some thinking, I decided to help them build a new house with better features. Four hours later, we were finished.

Giving the pigs a tour, they were crying with joy. All three pigs screamed, "Hooray!" and got along as a big happy family. Lesson learned!

Chloe Millard (11)
The Costello School, Basingstoke

THE GIANT SCORPION

I was striding through the desert until I bumped into a giant scorpion. It said, "Come on, hop on my back!" It sounded so encouraging that I hopped up on its back immediately.
We ran into a cobra that was twice the size of me. It tried to attack us, but luckily I jumped away. The scorpion and the cobra quickly started to fight. I ran away.
I soon arrived at a stream, so I followed it. Eventually, the stream led me to the village where Grandma lived. I looked for her house to give her the fruit I had.

Elliot Wilson (11)
The Costello School, Basingstoke

THE WOLF

I did it to survive, it's not like I wanted to kill the pigs. It's not what they deserved. They did nothing wrong, I just had to. I had no choice
You see, you'll have to forgive me, but I made a deal with Little Red Riding Hood a little while ago. Because she helped me learn how to hunt for fish, I had to repay her one day. When she told me that the 'disgusting' - as she called them - little pigs had started building houses on her land, I knew what I had to do, otherwise, she'd kill me.

Isla Waugh-Bacchus (11)
The Costello School, Basingstoke

A FORGOTTEN SPIDER

A forgotten spider was all sad and sorrowful. He wanted revenge on the internet, the world! He found the internet box. In an instant, he bit the wires. Electrocuted, I thought he was dead, but he struggled and then stood up in pain. He was fixed by evil scientists and then the hyper-mecha evil spider was born. He went on to rule the world, but was destroyed when the humans rebelled.

Many died, but some lived, so beware. I am telling you the fate of the human race. Listen to what I tell you. The future awaits.

Giacomo Sordon (12)
The Costello School, Basingstoke

MEDUSA

All I wanted to do was be normal, but because I accidentally turned people into stone, I wasn't allowed. I wanted to protect people and save them but all they saw in me was evil. They wanted to kill me and they always thought I was going to turn them into stone. No one ever trusted me. My ability to turn people into stone ruined my chance of actually being in a society with anyone. No one wanted anything to do with me just because they thought I was evil - but I never wanted to be evil. They forced me.

Julia Borowczyk (11)
The Costello School, Basingstoke

THE THREE BILLY GOATS GRUFF

Once upon a time, there lived three goats who lived in a beautiful daisy field, but one day they had the biggest shock of their lives. Everything had burned down!
Now they had nothing to eat except for the grass. But not all of the grass was good - some of it was as black as the night sky, some of it was as hot as lava.
The worst thing was, there was perfectly good grass across the haunted bridge. It was guarded by a huge green swamp monster. No one had ever crossed the bridge and come back alive.

Caitlin Mutlow (11)
The Costello School, Basingstoke

SHREK AND DONKEY

Once upon a time, an ogre, Shrek, and his sidekick, Donkey, ran up to the royal palace to steal the crown from the king. They climbed through the window and snuck up to the crown room. Shrek put the crown on his bald, green head. He then tied up the king, put the queen in the cupboard and tied her to the wall. He locked the door and ate the key. He chucked the king out of the window into the raging sea. Then he had a feast, where he married the pretty princess and lived happily ever after.

Ryan Tillotson (12)
The Costello School, Basingstoke

SLEEPING BEAUTY

Once upon a time, there was a happy little boy named Joy. It was his birthday party. The only person not invited was the evil maid.

Without an invitation, she arrived with a wand and a terrible idea. The king and queen were hugging the child when the maid cursed the boy. The curse was that he would die at the age of fifteen.

A few years later, he was wandering around the castle. He found a squirrel which bit him. He fell down on the spot. He could not be cured, so the king gave the maid the throne.

Jeron Thottungal (11)
The Costello School, Basingstoke

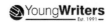

THE FAMOUS PIG AND THE JEALOUS PIG

One day, there was a famous pig and a jealous pig. One day, the jealous pig got so jealous, he decided he was going to ruin the famous pig. He was going to frame him; he could become popular instead of the famous pig.

But what would he frame him for? He decided to trash a park. He went to the store to buy some eggs and toilet paper. He waited for it to get dark, so no one would catch him.

He ruined the whole park! Then he wrote a note, blaming the famous pig and then ran away!

Addi Beaumont (12)
The Costello School, Basingstoke

MY LOVE

There stood a man I no longer knew. "Why are you doing this?!" I cried.

"Control!" He sounded evil, cold!

What had I done to deserve this? Panic filled me yet I was empty. I should never have fallen for that helpless face and inviting eyes. My protector, my shield, my love, had betrayed me, leaving me defenceless.

"Any last words?"

He was so heartless. His perfect features exposed a lack of emotion. I was stupid. I should've seen it coming.

"They say keep your friends close but your enemies closer. So where, my love, should I have kept you?"

Sydney Dukelow-Saxon (14)

The FitzWimarc School, Rayleigh

MONSTER

"It really was the only way," he stated. "I'm sorry."
Tears clogged up her eyes. Kneeling on the floor, frozen in time, she stared at the blood-covered blade as the life within her began to fade. The fear gripped her as her whole body shivered. "Monster," she muttered as her final breath escaped into the air.
"Actually, my name's Clarice," he said, grinning ear to ear. Well, until he turned around to see the haunted eyes of a young teenager. Hesitantly he put the knife down, looked up, and saw the flash of a camera's light. He was caught.

Khira Robinson (12)
The FitzWimarc School, Rayleigh

HER

It was never me. Never. Always *her*. Her perfect hair, her perfect grades, her perfect smile with her perfect red lipstick. Everything I envied. No one ever took notice of *me*. She once looked at me, however. Fear swam in her eyes; tears streamed down her face.

"Why so sad?" An evil grimace spread across my face.

Something red was oozing from her chest. Ruining her perfect white blouse. Blood pumping from her heart: running down to the floor, just like her tears.

Tossing the knife to the side, I watched the life slowly leave her once bright blue eyes.

Charlotte Kelleher (13)
The FitzWimarc School, Rayleigh

BEHIND CLOSED DOORS

He's everywhere. Billboards, buses, he's even on yoghurt pots. He walks around so entitled, as if everyone loves him so much. I mean, they do. I don't understand why, but they do.

I just want people to see what he's like behind closed doors, how he acts when nobody's around. I need one person, just one, to believe me. But they won't. No one believes me. Not even my parents believe that their golden child's capable of doing what he does. I mean, why would they? I'm only the villain in this story. The sibling that 'went insane'.

Lorna Quince (14)
The FitzWimarc School, Rayleigh

VICTORY

Finally, I was about to win. The building was turned to rubble by the celebrity's strength. But being pinned by machinery makes it difficult to finish your scene.

While the hero was stuck in a mousetrap, my visor would make the champion of this city into my pet. Information crashed into his head, destabilising his mind and losing the ability to speak.

I couldn't help but laugh at the imbeciles who'd bested me a thousand times screaming in terror of me. Or it was just his brain cells burning, not important. I'd keep winning forever. I'd live like a king.

Tristan Barker (14)

The FitzWimarc School, Rayleigh

19/10/1999

"Mummy, can we play hide-and-seek, please?"
"Of course, I don't see any harm in that. But only one game, then bed."
Excitedly, my children ran off down the dark blood-splattered hallway to hide. I counted to thirty. When I was finished, everything was silent and I started to search for them.
Later, I heard footsteps upstairs in the loft and I saw two shadows. Children's shadows. They screamed.
Blue and red lights flashed outside my house. I wiped the blood off my hands. I didn't want them to go back to their family.

Aimee Moores (12)
The FitzWimarc School, Rayleigh

THE MAN IN THE SHADOWS

Gasping for air, they woke to see themselves confined in a weary, wooden box. They turned only to come face-to-face with you, your hands sealed tightly in leather gloves that gently rested on a bloody shovel.

"You should have been quicker." Your manic laughter rang in their ears as you slammed the lid of the box shut. Their pitiful screams rang out before being drowned out as you shovelled mud onto the lid.

As they woke up screaming, you chuckled. The moonlight reflected off the shovel as you waited by a lamp post, its dim glow casting your shadow.

Zoe Webb (14)
The FitzWimarc School, Rayleigh

IT'S NOT CRICKET

James was already an established star cricketer at Rayleigh. Today, all eyes focused on his brother Ben's debut for Hadleigh, when they'd face each other.

It didn't disappoint. The crowd were gripped as the ball flew through the sky, glistening in the sunshine. Then, just as James hit the ball, it exploded in his face.

Screams pierced the air from all directions. Had talented, skilful James been killed? I could hear Ben shouting his innocence but it was falling on deaf ears.

No one had noticed their sister, Jenny, switching the ball!

Luke Gould (13)
The FitzWimarc School, Rayleigh

DOWNTOWN CHICAGO

As the police sirens blared, Maximus Val Johnson ran until he couldn't hear them anymore. This was all a massive misunderstanding.

Maximus was a 24-year-old male who stood six feet three inches tall. He had silky black hair, slicked back, and piercing blue eyes. He had just robbed a bank for 20 million in diamonds and taken 29 hostages.

The thing they didn't know, was that the notorious crime boss Devino Nucci had threatened to kill his parents as he was in debt and couldn't pay on time. He was forced. But would the cops believe him?

Brendon Pasipangodya (12)
The FitzWimarc School, Rayleigh

HERO OR VILLAIN?

Heroes don't know anything! They're all, "I am here. Look at me, I'm amazing." Get over yourself! I'll show you heroes can be villains. You just have to see the true picture.

Walking down the street with my head down, I saw a hero in an alley, shouting at a civilian because he got in the way of a mission. "Just talk to the poor lad!" I shouted.

The hero turned around, he had bloodthirst in his eyes. Yet I'm the villain because I want to get rid of these monsters. Pathetic. What I did next was unforgivable...

Brooke Nicole Webb (13)
The FitzWimarc School, Rayleigh

THE BASEMENT

It was one afternoon when I noticed my first victim. The key was placed into the keyhole and *bang!* The door smashed open. When the door was closed, I saw a seven-year-old girl walking in. My plan began.

The girl walked toward the basement after I mimicked her mum shouting. I thought about my meal. When the door opened, I got behind her and, as she turned around, I slowly put my bloody and bruised arms towards her neck and *crack!*

I was left with a body with a snapped neck. Immediately, I knelt and gobbled up every organ inside.

Reece Cooper (12)
The FitzWimarc School, Rayleigh

GUILT

I sat up, straight as a needle, and slowly crept downstairs. I switched the lever on the kettle. I waited for a moment, then it whistled dissonantly. I made myself a tea and sat down cosily on my sofa.

I turned to reach for the remote and pressed the button. The sound of static went right through me. I changed the channel and watched it precisely. Paying attention to the nuances.

I wanted to distract myself from the guilt. The regret. The invisible shackles of regret pulled me down every day and night. I just wished I didn't kill her.

Freya Bourdon (13)
The FitzWimarc School, Rayleigh

AT THE PARK

One Sunday afternoon, Miranda's mother took her to the local playground as a treat. Miranda ran over the slide while her mum, Shelly, sat on a park bench.

Shelly pulled out her phone and peered at her screen. Around twenty minutes later, Shelly looked up from her device. She searched for Miranda but she could not spot her. She heard a scream coming from the trees.

Hesitantly, she stood up and walked toward the trees. As she got to the opening, she saw someone lying in a pool of blood. She screamed. It was Miranda's dead body.

Taya Evans (12)
The FitzWimarc School, Rayleigh

NO WAY BACK

I could not turn back now. The damage had already been done. Lanterns hung off the walls, flickering on and off constantly. The screams of my victim filled my head as I chuckled to myself at the pain I had caused.

I felt an icy cold hand slowly grasp upon my shoulder, tightening its grip gradually. It jolted me back and glared with his soul-destroying eyes, as if he wanted to slit my throat clean open.

He twisted my arm 'til it snapped and pierced his claws through my face, leaving me defenceless on the ground. This was my payback.

Amy Gould (13)
The FitzWimarc School, Rayleigh

SORRY

I had to make up for what I had done! I felt terrible. I couldn't believe I had poisoned someone ten years ago because I was so angry with them for lying to me.

After ten years in prison, I'd realised I needed to find Emily's parents to apologise for what I did to their daughter. Had her parents started a new life after the devastating thing I did?

After lots of searching, I found them, in Nottinghamshire. I set off early, I had to meet them, I had to explain. Why didn't people believe I had changed?

Evie Francis (12)
The FitzWimarc School, Rayleigh

THE BODY SNATCHER

The clock struck twelve. I crept through the graveyard gates. Nothing stirred, dead silence.

Getting my rusty spade out, I began to dig at Plaque 34. Tomas Jones was the Mayor of Swansea but was tragically assassinated by my good friend Cecil. This was payback for not helping the poor.

My new job was much more rewarding, plenty of cash in my pockets. The doctor would be happy with this delivery. It was a gruesome job but it was all in the name of science, so to speak. Oh, wasn't vengeance sweet?

Emily Duckworth (11)
The FitzWimarc School, Rayleigh

FROM SCREAMS TO SILENCE

It was all for her. Everything, from the smoke-filled skies to the wave of terror I sent running through the dying city; from the screams to the silence, from fire to ice. I did it all for her.

That was always the plan, and my plans never failed. That was until this one. The one that didn't work. The one that left me to the clouds, leaving me to watch the world I loved burn to ashes because of me.

But of course, he had to come in and save the day, like always. That should've been me.

Anna Louise Reynolds (16)

The FitzWimarc School, Rayleigh

MURDERER

I'm insane... I couldn't believe what I did. Last night, I murdered someone. Jack Davies was his name. He got me excluded, so he had to pay.

I ran home and locked all the doors. Suddenly, sirens wailed outside my house. They barged down the door and arrested me. I was going to be thrown in jail for twenty-five years.

I couldn't do that kind of time. My friend broke me out. We were on the run. We were being chased by police. I had a gun; I shot. I had returned to my villainous ways.

Billy Jay (12)
The FitzWimarc School, Rayleigh

SHE'S TWISTED

Her heart filled with joy, his filled with fear. She looked at her crazed smile in the reflection of her favourite knife pointed towards his chest; he couldn't get away. She almost burst out laughing at this thought, but seeing the terror in his eyes satisfied her enough.

Pressing down into his chest, draining the life out of him, feeling pleasure from the ideas about what she was going to do to his lifeless body. Sitting on the floor with his body, she took her biggest razor and began.

Emilia Agathangelou (13)
The FitzWimarc School, Rayleigh

FLIPPED

"Argh!" Frodo staggered back, clutching his hand. His fingers parted and Sam saw a stump where his finger should have been.

"Master Frodo, where's the ring? Did it take it? Frodo? Frodo? Frodo?"

Frodo was swaying right and left, his eyes closed. Suddenly, he vomited on the floor.

"Master, stay with me. Frodo! Frodo!"

Frodo had collapsed on the floor like a heap of clothes, his body twitching.

"I'm coming, Master Frodo, hang on."

Sam attempted to run across the bridge. At the same time, Frodo stood up, swayed and fell down into the chasm below.

"*Noo!*"

Theo Johnston (12)
The Fulham Boys School, London

MASON, THE WICKED ASSASSIN

Eaten by snails. Tortured until his last bone. As skinny as a shrimp. There was no escape to this horrendous survival until light blazed through the dungeons of the Liverpool prison. It was his friend.

"Come." His hiss was heard from Heaven.

A few minutes later, Mason escaped the hell he'd experienced. Three scrawny figures aimed their taser into his helpless body, but it was too late. Mason did what they called 'the impossible'. Whoever tried to escape the prison ended up in their deadly graves of doom. Mason finally smelled the air of freedom. It was time for assassination...

Hamza Rhouzzal (12)
The Fulham Boys School, London

DEATH: I AM A SAVIOUR

I still remember what they did. I was the first to be killed. The species they chose. They did this. Humans. I was the only one who could beat them, that's why they eradicated me. I take from them what they took from me. I'm fair. I keep the planet in order. Overpopulation isn't a thing. Without me, everyone would die, not just me. It's a burden to carry. I must make sure that nothing like this happens again. However, I'm failing. All because of them. It ends now...

Rufus Dixon (12)
The Fulham Boys School, London

WHY 7 ATE 9

7 was no different to any other number. They sat in their house as usual and brewed themselves a nice cup of tea. Single sugar. They finished their tea when suddenly there was a knock at the door. 7 opened it and saw 9 standing there, holding their best friend,10, hostage. 9 looked at 7 menacingly. 7 saw 9 and lunged at them. 7 knew that there was only a single way to win the fight. So 7 started to eat 9. Suddenly, 6 saw 7. 6 saw 7 eat 9. 6 screamed in terror and called the police!

Will George (12)
The Fulham Boys School, London

NEVER STOPPING

I'm so small, so insignificant. I practically don't exist. So lonely, so sad that all I ever wanted was someone who wouldn't ignore me. After years of loneliness, I grew intolerant. I needed them now, so I began to scour. Through my determined craze, I searched. Never stopping, never slowing, I spread from person to person, city to city, until just one friend was found. However, nobody loved me. They all tried to kill me and told me to stay away from them. They made me a villain.

I'm still looking and longing, small, insignificant and sad. I am COVID-19.

Izzy Roberts (13)
The King's School, Worcester

THE BURNING FIRE INSIDE ME

Finally, I was about to win. The small spark that I had started now morphed into a raging flame. I watched. Everything burned.

The piercing screams echoed through my bloody ears. An evil smile exposed my blackened teeth as my cut lips curled towards my broken nose.

Something wasn't right. My lips returned and formed a low, broken frown. My heart shrivelled like a decaying leaf and turned as black as night. The horrified screams echoed through my ears once more and a salty wet tear appeared from my bloodshot eye.

I felt an emptiness inside. What had I done?

Tom Phillips (13)
The King's School, Worcester

THE NEW COOL

I never really belonged, even if my life from the outside seemed perfect. It was not. They said it was easy to fit in. They said I was weak. That's what they really thought of me. Also that I was never going to fit in.
Now it is cool not to fit in. They will never breathe again and all my troubles are gone. "It isn't good to be dead," they say, but who knows? They don't know what is good because being bad feels good.
Maybe I have found my calling. How can a dead person ever be heard?

Sophie Evans
The King's School, Worcester

DEATH

I have nothing to apologise for. Much like an accountant or a doctor, I'm simply doing my job. You cannot blame me. And besides that, I am, of course, freeing as many as I am condemning.

I guess, though, I do deserve the end I'm being faced with, to feel the things they've felt before. There's something strangely beautiful about the death of Death myself. I would laugh, if I could, if I was someone who could be amused. You expect me to apologise? Over my dead body.

Sophie Ruane (13)
The King's School, Worcester

DON'T BE FOOLISH; SOULTHIEF NEVER FAILS TO TAKE

Allow this clarification: I am one of those whom you shouldn't hide from. Fear me, it's normal, but don't foolishly believe you will outrun me or somehow remain unnoticed by me for your whole life, because it doesn't work like that, dear friend.

Once lived a child, composed, intelligent, who avoided me whenever possible. She evaded danger, eluded complications, slithered through my grasp countless times. However, one particularly dismally thunderous, sinister evening, I captured her, finally securing her.

Face pulled into a snarl, she attempted to escape, though attempting is futile. She struggled, but I, Soulthief, won. Like. Every. Time.

Maariyah Naseem (12)
The Madani Academy, Buckland

ROMANCING THE STAR

Thanos was born on Saturn's moon of Titan. Thanos was extremely powerful and resilient. "I, Thanos, will reclaim the last soul gem. Take what is mine! I will destroy this city! I know there will be a little goody-two-shoes waiting."
"Welcome to our world," Thor chuckled.
"You!" Thanos roared with frustration. "You're so weak, Thor, I will crush you and get what I'm here for." He crept warily closer with his powers. "Get up and fight for your precious city."
Thor was terrified and dropped the gem. The diamond, sat upon his finger, welded to a strangling band of gold.

Jannah Alam (15)
The Madani Academy, Buckland

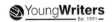

THE WICKED WITCH OF THE WEST

When you think of the great Wizard of Oz, what comes to mind? Powerful? Wise? Courageous? All words you're probably thinking of. Well, you'll be sad to know, the heroic act was *all a lie!*

My younger brother is a talentless, scheming traitor. Oz was rightfully to be mine, but that swine spun lies and silly magic tricks, exiling me to the west, making me 'The Wicked Witch of the West'.

Shocked? Yes, something they don't mention in the stories - erasing my darling brother's treachery and making me the villain. After all, we can't tarnish his perfect reputation, can we?

Afifa (12)
The Madani Academy, Buckland

MONSTER

The train chugged along, making a horrible screech against the metal track. It came to a sudden halt, indicating that I had arrived. Slowly getting off, I lifelessly trudged towards my waiting aunt.

Shame pooled within me as my aunt looked at me with extreme disappointment, repulsion, and something else I didn't want to decipher.

I know now that I did wrong but back then I didn't. Nobody helped me see the right path until I messed up. Until it was too late. My regret is all-consuming but useless; people don't see it. All they see is an irredeemable monster.

Amani (14)
The Madani Academy, Buckland

LOKI

My brother, Thor, is a hero. A good guy, unlike me. Everyone's always delighted to see him and, as soon as he arrives home to Asgard, he gets all the praise.

However, when I come over, all the death threats are made specifically for me. My brother's so-called 'Avenger' friends are absolutely loathsome. I despise having to see their faces on the paper and on what Midgardians (earthlings) call television.

I honestly wonder what it's like for people to like me. The only person that likes me is, well, myself. I doubt that anyone would ever love me.

Nayyara Islam (12)
The Madani Academy, Buckland

THROUGH THE YELLOW EYES

I looked at the girl in red. She didn't seem scared. The big white teeth and long pointy ears did not seem to bother her. Carefully, the girl approached.

A sudden realisation hit. I was not one, just like she was not one. We were one together. Me being her evil and darkness, her being the kind, cheerful girl everybody loved, whilst I was feared, chased out of my home and not shown any kindness, only hatred and weapons.

She backed away, feeling the same thing as I did and skipped merrily back into the woods where Grandma was.

Kayna Farrell (13)
The Roseland Academy, Tregony

DEAR METROPOLIS MUSEUM

Dear Metropolis Museum, I am Hope. I am writing to confess. I have stolen an artefact from your Egyptian exhibit: Cleopatra's staff.

I know, I know, you're probably wondering why I'm confessing. Well, let me tell you a little about myself. I was born in South Russia. I was trained by only the best, to steal the rarest of items.

My mother died when I was four and, as revenge, my father employed me to steal the rarest items from the people who killed my mother. Now, is your name Richard Fernando, by any chance? You hurt my mother. Idiot.

Reece Thwaites
The Whitstable School, Kent

HAUNTED

The house was covered in ivy, with cracked windows and stone dragons. The door was crooked and creaked as I opened it. I saw a never-ending spiral staircase. It twisted and turned, and dust covered my fingers as I touched the bannister.

At the top of the staircase, there was a door standing alone. I turned the door handle slowly. It clicked. My hand trembled as I pushed the door open.

There was a woman in a rocking chair. The woman turned to me. She had no shadow. Suddenly, she disappeared and I heard a piercing scream from the kitchen...

Phoebe McLean
The Whitstable School, Kent

A NOBODY

People think they know everything about me but the truth is there is much more. They just don't bother to look closer. Probably better that way.

Let me tell you a bit about who I am. I have lots of names, such as weirdo, rat, thief. I never knew my parents, so I don't really know who I am myself. Most people say I am a cheap pickpocket from New York but I am way more skilled.

I wouldn't call myself a villain yet. Sure, I have done some bad stuff. Who cares? Nobody to disappoint. No one at all.

Líadain Saxe-Traquair (12)
The Whitstable School, Kent

ILLUSION

Erroneous, false, fallacious myths cast across the world, like a magic wand without any contemplation. Forever labelled the villain.

"I am a god!" My raspy, agitated voice reverberated in my hollow lair. Empty, like me.

Growing up with an injudicious father who declares you unfilial, an outcast, from the day you were born. Two brothers, heroes to some. Murderers who killed our parents, in truth. Who cower from the consequences and inculpated me. Their ingenuous brother.

To the world, I was nothing. I was dead. From thereafter, I decided I would subdue them, for I am Hades. I wanted revenge.

Ruby Booth
The William De Ferrers School, South Woodham Ferrers

THE WITCH

Do you pity Hansel and Gretel? You shouldn't. Those little cretins flounced into my life and my heart jumped. I had a chance at redemption, to bring back my baby! The two ingredients I needed appeared right in front of me. Child-like innocence and undying love through blood.
Welcoming them in, they munched, crunched and licked my walls. I led them towards the kitchen, hoping to fatten them up - that way, they wouldn't be able to run away.
Next, they rushed over to the cauldron. This was it! Get my child back with one swift push. Then they pushed me.

Toby Booth
The William De Ferrers School, South Woodham Ferrers

URSULA

You see Ursula as a sea witch but do you know how she became so wicked? Ursula was a beautiful mermaid and made lots of potions. One day, one of her potions went wrong.

She was engaged to King Triton until her accident. He left her. Anger boiled up inside, exploding like the cauldron in front of her. Revenge was what she wanted. Revenge was what she got.

She tricked Ariel, taking her out of the sea. But Ariel met her 'sole'mate and got married. King Trident was alone. Vulnerable. Ursula tried becoming a mermaid again to win him back.

Evie Booth

The William De Ferrers School, South Woodham Ferrers

MALEFICENT

I was the perfect child until I was cursed. My younger sister took away my life. For that, she had to pay. Aurora, sweet and innocent. Aurora this, Aurora that.

I was forgotten. My life: miserable - then spectacular. An old witch I stumbled upon cursed me to be like her. Horrid powers and immortal life. At first, I was horrified. Then I had an idea. An idea for Aurora to pay for her actions.

I'd curse her.

It wasn't evil exactly, just a way of showing her how much she'd ruined my life. A perfect plan, except for the prince.

Amber Carver (14)
The William De Ferrers School, South Woodham Ferrers

QUEEN OF HEARTS

I hate the Mad Hatter! He tricked Alice into thinking that I stole the Cheshire cat from him. When I visited the blue caterpillar, somehow, he managed to distract all of my guards so Alice could steal the Cheshire cat.
When I got back and noticed he was gone, I got all my guards to search for my cat. When they returned, I saw him and he leapt out of my guard's arms and ran straight towards me.
I noticed on his collar it said his owner was the Mad Hatter. I screamed at my guards, "Off with his head!"

Maisie Smith (14)
The William De Ferrers School, South Woodham Ferrers

THE WICKED WITCH AND JAMES' FAMILY

"My family and I haven't done anything to you," cried James. Mary, the witch, got furious and hung him to the bloody walls. "Your family stole my money! I will poison them!" shouted Mary. She disappeared.

He could see his family in a cauldron. The witch teleported to James' house and pretended to be a maid. James cried, he could see everything that was going on through the cauldron.

The second day, the witch was preparing food and added poison. James' family ate the food and exploded! Pink blood went everywhere. The witch teleported back. She smiled, he'd died.

Michele Abbey (12)
The Wren School, Reading

DESTRUCTION

Albedo was experimenting on some potions to try and grow flowers from any random object. There were two green potions. Albedo picked up the green potion that was for his experiment. He mixed the green potion with the other pink potion. Nothing. Nothing!

Another failed experiment, thought Albedo. It was late, quite late, so Albedo went to bed but, before he did so, he drank the potion to see if anything had changed. Nope. So he left.

Later, his neck ached. He thought it was normal. Next thing he knew, he was destroying his town.

He'd drunk the wrong potion.

Mia Knox-Roberts (11)
The Wren School, Reading

LAST BREATH

It was one grim night as one lonely boy, named Jimmy, stared deep into the fire. His mother had passed away when he was small and he now lived with his foster family that he hated.

One night, as he stared into the fire, he heard his mother's whisper, "*Come!*" He suddenly got into the blazing flames. He woke up in a dimly lit cave. He saw his mother with a blank stare and emotionless eyes. But just as he was about to approach her, her arms suddenly creaked into a formidable creature, with raggedy flesh and bloodstained teeth. "*Aah!*"

Amal Nirmalkumar (11) & Fernando Ogbonna
The Wren School, Reading

ESCAPE FROM THE REAPER

He ran from the loud, distorting sounds behind him. He slowly looked back. His heart stopped suddenly. The reaper vanished, leaving only a puff of red smoke.

He sprinted to a great old tree and hid behind it. The echoes came from the barren, desolate tree: "*Stop trying, let it take you.*" Branches started to grow and circle around him. He could feel the tree stare at him.

He woke up and was relieved. He was safe! Then it occurred to him that everyone was gone. He carefully went outside and saw the reaper, the tree and the portal too.

Logan Codling (11)

The Wren School, Reading

THE MYSTERIOUS WITCH

One dark and precarious night, Lola's TV randomly turned on. "*A mysterious witch has a plan to kill the Queen. It's up to one of you to help and warn the Queen. Don't be shy! Help the lady out.*" The TV shut off.

Lola knew she must do something, so she headed for the woods. After walking for a while, Lola bumped into a tree with a door! She heard a loud cackle from inside and decided to knock on the door.

"Hello?" The door creaked open. "Why do you want to kill the Queen?"

She just laughed.

Admiah Sinclair (11)

The Wren School, Reading

WORDS OF THE WICKED

I was always the one in the mountains, never a part of the village. I sit on the edge of the highest cliff, watching the children. I was a bad girl, banished to solitude for my crimes. I remember that night, fifty nights ago, when the villagers chased me up the mountain, brandishing flaming torches. I remember the cold night air whistling past my face as I ran, further up, until I was touching the dark sky.

Now, I stand on the mountaintop, looking down, watching, waiting. The wind flurries as I begin my revenge. I smile. It's time.

Elvie Oakland (11)

The Wren School, Reading

PROJECT JOYKILL

It has been a tiring day and I can't believe I have lost to that dreaded Vino, who barged into my base and destroyed it. Now it's all dilapidated. I am going to show that hero scum my true power.

"Chronos, activate our power project."

"*Joykill activated.*"

"Thank you, Chronos." Now it's time to say hi to Vino, my old pal. "Well, hello there, my old pal, Vino. I have a surprise that will ruin your reign on the throne... Meet my child, Joykill."

"Golgshadow, stop this now. You don't need to do this."

"Say hi, Joykill."

"*Hello, Vino.*"

Luke Winrow (12)
Thornhill Community Academy, Thornhill

THE ENEMY

He stormed through the great hall. His cape was ripped and seasoned with blood splatters. He narrowed his eyes at the sight of his enemy.

Opposing him was a woman in a golden costume, it shimmered in the chandelier. The crystals of it taunted the audience, spiralling and threatening to drop. The crowd was large, women in elegant, stately gowns and men in matching suits twice as extravagant.

Quickly, he drew his sword. He scratched it against the floor, making a monstrous noise. He scurried across the auditorium, pulling his sword in front of himself. Black bile flooded his vision.

Amber Norman
Thornhill Community Academy, Thornhill

GLOWING EYES

I look towards the clock. Then back and forth, from the clock to the light. My heart fills with realisation. Ten seconds left. I look around and search for those green eyes, but they're nowhere to be seen.

Suddenly, the lights rapidly flicker. I turn around again, to finally see the sight I wanted. Those glowing emerald eyes. They repay me a look, staring deep into the amethyst depths of mine.

A smile stains my wretched face while their beautiful face fills with horror. Our glowing eyes maintain contact. They know that vengeance is coming for them, my vengeance.

Aamirah Maniar (11)
Thornhill Community Academy, Thornhill

MY MONSTER WITHIN

"I didn't mean to kill them!" Words spluttered out of my mouth like I was the one dying. The nerves crept in, getting worse with every breath I took, feeling as if there was a limited amount of oxygen left.

That was how it started. Living hell. But the rush of adrenaline coursing through my body made me long for more.

Screeching tyres, a car door slammed shut. A mysterious, shadowed figure approached me. His piercing, knife-like eyes darted toward me quicker than I have ever seen before.

I saw a blade. The next thing I knew, he was dead.

Summer Fox (11)
Thornhill Community Academy, Thornhill

IN THE EYES OF THE VILLAINS

Everyone asks, why do murderers kill? Why would they do despicable things? Don't they have decency?

But that's how it starts. To get a person to become a killer, you need to drive them to a point where they've had enough. And that's what happened with me.

They drove me crazy in ways I couldn't imagine. Bullied me in ways that weren't acceptable. So I came back and showed them all how it feels to be scared to live in your own home or even walk on the streets. And that's how I became one of the country's Most Wanted.

Sumayyah Hussain (14)

Thornhill Community Academy, Thornhill

FALLEN SURGEON

Dak, a surgeon, begins to have headaches and they last for over a month. To eradicate the pain, Dak takes cocaine. He eventually gets caught and gets sentenced to five years. Once he's served his years, Dak starts to rage as he believes he did nothing wrong. Dak begins to make his move, by removing the faces of his patients, just like the people he sees without medication. He then uses the drug Scopolamine to make people commit murder and get caught.

Dak, in his final act, turns himself in. Guilt fills his mind as he gets the death sentence.

Janos Tauz (11)
Thornhill Community Academy, Thornhill

REVENGE IS BEST SERVED DEAD!

Black Swan, my most treasured possession. I looked after my crew. My life was perfect. But I took on the wrong shipmate. He worked well, then the traitor killed me in my sleep. He took control of my ship, my wife; they had children together.

I'm the ghost that haunts this ship. I terrorise him, and the brats, every night. He killed me and stole my life. I was nice to him. That wretch of a wife should've killed herself, rather than be his. So much for love.

I live alone. I killed them all. Revenge is best served dead.

Daisy Bramley (12)
Thornhill Community Academy, Thornhill

NO REMORSE

I wiped the blade clean, regrets flooding my heart, and I kept asking myself one question: why? It puzzled me every time I asked myself. I constantly wondered how I'd got myself into this terrible life.

I poured myself a glass of whiskey and continued to fill my head with unanswerable questions. I tried to remember each victim and tried to feel just a bit of remorse. I thought of their families and the sorrow I'd brought them.

I felt a welling up in my eyes. No matter how hard I tried, I just couldn't cry.

Olivia Wilson (13)
Thornhill Community Academy, Thornhill

MARY TUDOR BEHIND THE SCENES

It happened. I was the Queen of England. I exited the carriage about 8:15am. As I awaited my royal advisor, my body was quaking and my knees were shaking. Everyone knew I would be great, but everything took a turn as I was holding onto my throne by a straw.

Nervously, I threw my sister into jail and then I viciously murdered anyone who went against me - especially if they were part of the Church of England. I have my regrets though, some of which can be found in my next chapter.

Faye Longley (12)
Thornhill Community Academy, Thornhill

WARNING TO WANDA

"You're here to end the Avengers?" Wanda questioned.

"No, I'm here to warn them..." Ultron's raspy voice made the twins' breath cut short.

"What are you talking about?" Pietro's timid voice asked.

"They are in grave danger, a Titan called Thanos plans to wipe out 50% of the universe. Get the Avengers and-"

A familiar shield wedged into Ultron's vibranium chest.

"You're coming with us," Tony barked.

Wanda stalked around the Avengers, exclaiming, "He was trying to-"

"Not right now!" Natasha asserted.

"You're all gonna die..." the forgotten robot said, his eyes slowly flickering out. Everyone stared, silence drowning them.

Martha Tweddell (12)

Thorp Academy, Ryton

GROGU

Some say that the real villain is the one that operates in the shadows. In the shadow of the valleys of Vandor, filled with fury, Grogu accuses Luke of killing Yoda. The force tells him this, definitively. Grogu catapults a rock into Luke's skull. Grunting, Luke stares at Grogu, dismayed. "Grogu, please! What's wrong?" Luke stutters, aghast.

Grogu continues catapulting rocks, disregarding Luke's pleading. Luke turns to run to his ship, desperate not to hurt Grogu. Grogu sees his only opportunity and ends Luke's life. Luke's soul surrenders to the force.

I'd better head back, Mando's probably worried, Grogu thinks.

Evan Casson (11)
Thorp Academy, Ryton

QUEEN OF HEART-LESS

Tears rolled down the girl's face, ruining make-up that her mother made her wear. "You chopped her head off!" the princess sobbed, clinging to her mother.

"Do you want to be queen, child?" her mother demanded, possessed by maniacal fury.

Nodding frantically, the little girl rubbed away her tears, sniffling.

"Then you do as I say," the queen snapped, pushing the princess to the floor. "If you want to be queen, you follow my example - make them fear you." The older woman's voice was harsh. Cruel. "I've been meaning to dispose of your father; you can do it for me."

Isabel McGuire (13)
Thorp Academy, Ryton

ON THE OTHER HOOK

He's back. Peter Pan's back and he's kidnapped more children. My heart tries to leap free, but it's encased by prison bars of bone. Every time he returns, trouble isn't far behind.

This time he's brought a lass. We all know what happened to the last 'replacement mother'. I stroke my hook, fretting. She doesn't know what he's planning. I have to do something.

But what if Peter has warned them about me? And, if he hasn't, a hook-handed, bearded pirate will just unnerve them. I shake this off. I have to try, for Grace's sake, for my daughter's sake.

Eva Bainbridge (13)
Thorp Academy, Ryton

NEVER-ENDING GORY

William Afton, that's me. Infamous, wanted murderer. They say I'm guilty, but what of? I was just a businessman; dealing in pain and terror.

The twinkles of panic in children's eyes brings me the purest form of joy I've ever known. I kill them one by one. Bodies never to be found - stored in animatronic machines. Their corpses swallowed by mechanical bodies, souls hidden from prying eyes. Never to be spoken of again.

But now, their souls come for vengeance. They've come to take their vindictiveness out upon me. Now, there's no outrunning karma - a painful death awaits me!

Tiffany Bisset (13)
Thorp Academy, Ryton

BEHIND THE PRETTY FACE

Happily ever after, *ha*. Did they really think it was over, they could just kiss and *poof*, the problems are gone?
"Mirror, mirror on the wall, show the real story to us all."
It all started when I first went into Snow White's life. Obviously, it is not easy being a stepmother but she made it ten times harder. This just shows she's more than just a pretty face. She's trouble!
After everything she put me through, it's time for payback. I never meant any harm at first. I wish I could say the same now.

Elyssa Campbell
Tower Learning Centre Independent School, Blackpool

SLEEP PARALYSIS

I woke up to the sound of a chilling rattle at the corner of my room. The deep drone of scraping slithered down my spine. My eyes opened in the bleak moonlight, steering themselves from left to right, tracing my expanse.
Abruptly, The noise ceased. I tried to reach for a light switch but my body lay limply. Louder and louder, the rattle cooed again, hollowly beckoning me.
With my heart bellowing fearfully, I shakily caught my breath. "It's alright," I told myself reassuringly. But, before I could continue, my eyes met with a stark figure, looming balefully over me.

Imani Owade (13)

Towers School & Sixth Form Centre, Kennington

GUILTY

Crimson guilty liquid drew from the body as the breath faded to nothing but white noise. Patches of red covered me, a sign of conscience, but an overriding feeling of success floated through my body as I strutted calmly from the soulless body, smirking to myself jubilantly.
My breathing hitched as I saw a blue and white light flashing vigorously through the night sky. Fleeing from the scene, I stumbled over a twig. Eyes reaching, trying to get free from my socket. My strategic, panicking brain was waiting for the voices, which were less than metres away, to subside.

Amber Kennedy (13)
Towers School & Sixth Form Centre, Kennington

WHO IS THE HERO?

I could see the light of the stars gleaming on his sword, praising him, like a spotlight highlighting a performer. Cheers echoed throughout the crowd, glimpsing the hero that'd saved their village. He had destroyed their enemy and had a blade as a trophy.

I was there. I knew what happened. I saw the moonlight reflecting off his newly earnt crown like it was made of liquid gold. The people were proud of him. They cherished his victory.

But they ignored the consequence. The city caught in ashes behind them. The city I loved. The city I tried to protect.

Shiloh Villion (13)
Towers School & Sixth Form Centre, Kennington

HERO OR VILLAIN?

They take and they kill. They loot and they pillage. And yet they wonder why we cry. Cry out for freedom, for a better life. Free from their authoritarian control. We wished for a hero, yet many lost hope.

But I've learnt, sometimes if you want something done, you've got to do it yourself. So I fled, in search of a saviour, only to return alone. Alone yet stronger.

I fought for those who couldn't fight for themselves. Now the only satisfaction I find is the haunting of their screams. Screams I once recognised, for they were my very own.

Penny Williams
Towers School & Sixth Form Centre, Kennington

REVENGE

I languish in my lonely underwater cave, swaying with revenge, thinking about the dancing mermaids. The tentacles sway in my sight as I imagine having a beautiful tail like them. Singing the mermaid siren, I remember the wicked tricks they played on me.

Floating gently, I stared into the deep ocean, trying my best to look as stunning as the gorgeous mermaids. What had I done wrong? I weep in my cave, waiting for my chance. My new life.

Then revenge overwhelms me. The beautiful sea-green tail and her elegant red hair taunt me. This is my sign.

Katie Woods
Towers School & Sixth Form Centre, Kennington

FAIREST OF THEM ALL

The house creaks and moans. Doors squeak in the silence. No one was there and yet shadows walked across the floor. A shriek of an owl penetrates the heart of the house. It wakes her up.

The fairest of them all shoots up and looks into the darkness. Fourteen eyes stare back. Screaming in horror, she faints. The eyes drag her to another room, lit with only one lightbulb in the middle.

They place her under it, to look at her, to forever be displayed as the fairest of them all. Her hopes drop; she was trapped forever.

Karis Davies (13)

Towers School & Sixth Form Centre, Kennington

THE BEAST

Icy rain fell from the sky as the wind roared across the land. He stood there, shaking with anger and declaring, "She doesn't love me. She loves it. It. The beast. I am so handsome and strong. I don't see why she doesn't want me. I love her more than anyone."

His eyes turned red and green in anger and jealousy. "This will be my revenge on the beast!"

He started to sharpen the knife and imagined piercing the beast's back. He laughed. "Belle will soon be mine."

Molly James (11)

Towers School & Sixth Form Centre, Kennington

ENVY IS BEST SERVED COLD

There he was. He was crying his eyes out. His mother was gone. As she lay there, lifeless, in her living room, I wondered how the young, helpless boy was just sitting there.
He wept and stared deep into my soul with his dark, puddled eyes, so long it left a deep, unfillable hole. The body was cold. He touched it and kept shaking it, hoping his mother would wake up. But she didn't.
I felt bad. But what he didn't know was worse - I had done this. I had killed my wife in cold, envious blood.

Gracie Hopper (14)
Towers School & Sixth Form Centre, Kennington

POPPY, BE MINE

I'd never noticed Poppy's eyes were green. She still had roses braided into her glossy black hair and her skin was waxy. Her dress was marked from the glimmering beads of cold sweat on her chest.

Such a shame the struggle bent the petals before she got to prom. She still looked pretty, though. The bouquet of flowers was still in my hand, with the blood-covered knife concealed once again.

Why couldn't she just say yes to me? Why make it so difficult? Why ruin the night for us both? It could've been so easy! Never mind. Prom's overrated anyway.

Imani Waseem (14)

Trinity Academy Grammar, Sowerby Bridge

THE TRIGGER

As I was about to pull the trigger, for the first time in my life I felt guilt. Why was this happening? My hands were shaking and my heart pounding, this wasn't normal.

As I looked at his face, his expression made it worse. He was staring in shock. I could definitely tell. All of a sudden, anger took over my body and I pulled the trigger.

I quickly turned around and saw everyone staring, judging me. The police sirens were flooding the eerie silence. People started to cry and scream; I'd never felt so blessed. I killed them all.

Eleanor Baines (14)

Trinity Academy Grammar, Sowerby Bridge

YOU'LL BE THE DEATH OF ME

Nana always told me, "Family is all you have. Don't ever take your family for granted!" I guess I waited too long to listen to her advice. She'd skin me alive if I came back.
It is too late now to beg for her forgiveness; the deed is done. I'd slit his throat. I'd slit his throat right there and then. If I am being honest with myself, I'd enjoyed it. Every second, I'd been loving it.
We often joke that brothers only stop fighting when one dies. In my case, it is true. And I truly loved every second.

Nusayba Zaman (13)
Trinity Academy Grammar, Sowerby Bridge

HOT SUGAR

Vanilla melted in the hot pan that was encased in fire. Herbs were hanging off the wall, and the work surface was covered in flour. There was the faint smell of burning caramel and a door open leading to the basement.
Walking further, you can see a mirror and a room, dimly lit. Do you walk in? It suddenly goes dark and you are strapped to a chair.
"Welcome to my wonderland!" a voice whispers from behind your ear. Hot caramel drips onto your arms and legs and you wince in pain. "You're in for a surprise."

Amelia Czapiewska (14)
Trinity Academy Grammar, Sowerby Bridge

MY REASON

Blood. It's my coping mechanism. It listens to me. When I tell it to spill, it spills. But it hasn't always been my escape. My virtue.

I once had a weakness. And oh, what a weakness it was. It was a weakness you craved. It was amazing. Incredible. She was beautiful.

So, as I stand here, watching the colour drain from each and every one of their faces. I picture her. My beloved weakness. It's gone now. She's gone now.

I was once against all things evil. I was once good. I was once happy. I'm not anymore...

Aliya Rahman (13)
Trinity Academy Grammar, Sowerby Bridge

PATIENCE

I never really belonged on Earth. I was bullied a lot by a girl called Cathy and her group of pink Barbies. I loved anything to do with black and blood. Because of this, the pink Barbies started to call me Death.

At first, I had no problem with this, until I started to hear it every minute of every day. Then it got really annoying.

It all changed when I met Megan. She made me who I am now. And when she did, I decided I wanted to get a little bit of revenge. It was worth the wait...

Karlina Buse (11)
Trinity Academy Grammar, Sowerby Bridge

HERE'S TO YOU

I am here today to announce to you that malicious rebels have attacked our utopia. I am very upset and distressed by this unfortunate news. However, when there is hardship, we must prevail.

Fortunately, some rebels were captured and are being publicly executed. Their families are going to be our slaves to repair the damage that has been done.

I am the law. I am the judge. I am, most certainly, the executioner.

Kamran Azam (14)
Trinity Academy Grammar, Sowerby Bridge

THE SLASHER BY NIGHT

I just finished slaughtering two men in their own homes, then ate their organs. I don't do it because they taste nice, I do it because it makes me feel normal again. Well, as normal as it gets for a cannibal like me, who'll slaughter any human they come across.

"Anyways, that's the note the killer left after he killed those two men last night," Dave said to the police captain.

Then Captain Rodger exclaimed, "We need to get this guy soon or he'll murder everyone in the city!"

Bob replied by saying, "They're calling him the Midnight Slasher."

Kegan Bell (13)

Trinity Academy Halifax, Holmfield

THE UNDERWORLD GOD'S PROCLAMATION

In fire and sin, I was born and then it's Lord I was delegated to be. My father, Kronos, devoured me and my brother, Zeus, freed me - only to tether me to a place of divine punishment and judgment everlasting.

I am Hades and I'm the God of the Underworld. Isn't it ironic? How a power forced upon someone such as mine can have such dire consequences for the vain, egotistical fools who 'ever so graciously' bestowed the power upon you in the first place?

They loathe me. They fear me. They wanted a monster. So a monster they'll get!

Rowan Adam Aspin (16)
Trinity Academy Halifax, Holmfield

CHRISTMAS PRESENTS TO CHRISTMAS PRESENT

Joyful music played in the background. The delicious taste and smell of beef filled the air. I stood alone, solitary. Then someone caught my eye, it was love at first sight.

A beautiful vision was standing a breath away from me. Her name was Belle but our relationship wasn't to last forever. Belle was demanding. She wanted a bracelet. I refused to waste my money on silly jewellery.

I wished that Belle understood that love didn't have to be shown with money. Unfortunately, she didn't agree. She left and I was devastated.

Katie McEvoy (15)
Trinity Academy Halifax, Holmfield

NO MORE BELLES AT CHRISTMAS

It was a crisp winter's day. I could hear the church bells ringing and everything was covered in white snow. I arrived at work and had just started working when my girlfriend burst through the door.

She begged me to come with her to a graveyard for a few minutes. I didn't want to but I agreed. We sat on a bench together.

Then she said, "I have been replaced with a golden idol."

I was annoyed! My girlfriend said that I cared about money more than her! She broke our engagement and left me. She broke my heart.

Yaseen Sakallah (14)
Trinity Academy Halifax, Holmfield

DOWNFALL

I waited for years, I waited by the moor's side for uncountable years. Yet the one thing I desired most went to Cassio, Michael Cassio! That man didn't deserve a single penny, still, he got the attention I deserved.

I can't stand that moor. He deserves a downfall to Hell. I, Iago, shall take my wrath on him, take away what he loves most. And I know who... his beloved wife.

Her death will eat him inside. Just to watch him suffer is my most wanted thing. All the ways I can make him sorrowful... Death will meet him soon.

Axel Rivers (14)
Trinity Academy Halifax, Holmfield

MYSTERY TRAIN MURDER

I was having a day off work just to get my mind around something else. I was on the train, it felt like hours since I'd got on.

Soon, I felt blood dripping onto my forehead, so I warned everyone to be aware. Seconds later, I felt a sharp pain go into my back and I collapsed straight onto the floor. All I could see and hear were people screaming and running. Moments later, my eyes closed but this time I could only hear gunshots. As well as people screaming. At that very second, the train went totally quiet.

Keeley Hambrey (13)
Trinity Academy Halifax, Holmfield

THE WINTER DOWNFALL

White flakes fell from the sky. Snow, it was glittering down to the ground. Setting the fire up like every year, yet even the fire seemed to freeze up. I left the wood next to the fire just in case.

I then went to the shop, leaving Mom and Sam alone. I got to the shops and felt for my wallet, nothing. I ran back home and got to the turn of my street and walked slower.

I paused. An orange glow illuminated the street. I stopped and smiled. White flakes fell from the sky: ashes. It was sparking down.

Julia Gonera (13)
Trinity Academy Halifax, Holmfield

THE SAD STORY OF LADY TREMAINE

I feel so bad for Cinderella, I shouldn't have treated her like I did. I did it for a reason. She was as stunning as a white swan in the water. She got everything I ever wanted from him. Love. Affection. Attention.

I just wanted to make her feel as miserable as I felt. I tore up her beautiful dress to make her feel as ugly as I felt. I worked her hard so he never saw her. Maybe without her, he'd love me more.

But he didn't give me the love I wanted. He ignored me. He loathed me.

Chanelle Clutton (13)

Trinity Academy Halifax, Holmfield

I WILL BE KING

It was a miserable day. I'd had enough of my brother and nephew by the end of it. Me and my brother had an argument because I really wanted to be king and he would not allow it.

Did I really not deserve to be king? Not only had I been arguing with my brother, my nephew was also laughing at me, saying I'd never be good enough.

It was time to take this matter into my own hands. I would be king! Tonight was the night. We were arguing again, so I decided to push him off that cliff.

Haarisah Ideson (12)
Trinity Academy Halifax, Holmfield

MURDER

It was a dark night. I lay there, thinking about everything. I was a child locked in an adult's body. I had no escape.
I could hear my stepmum. I thought she hated me. My foster carer was evil. I couldn't believe I was in this hell place. It was morning, I woke up to my mum screaming in my face. I was doing chores. I was fine.
Time to kill my social worker. She was telling my family to get rid of me. I got my hammer and jumped out across the road. It scared her and killed her.

Libby Condie (12)
Trinity Academy Halifax, Holmfield

THE QUEEN OF HEARTS

I was always the person to blame growing up. If I had something, Mirana had to have it too. She was always known as the prettier one, the smarter one, the one who should rule. She even got the title the White Queen to show her purity!
I will never forgive her for that night. The night she blamed me. The night that caused me to end up like this. She was greedy to eat that tart. But she is so flattering she got away with it! I may have the crown but I'm never treated like I deserve it.

Ferne Oxlade (12)
Trinity Academy Halifax, Holmfield

THE BRIBING OF THE SEA

I still haven't forgotten about what the King of the Ocean, Triton, did to me. This is Ursula, I am apparently the witch of the sea, the person that spent too long holding this secret: the real witch or warlock is King Triton himself.

He bribed me to keep my mouth shut about his secret behind rising to power. He was just a lonely little boy when I found him. I took him in and raised him for years. The next thing I knew, I was the witch of the sea and he was the new king.

Lola Carney Williams (13)
Trinity Academy Halifax, Holmfield

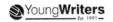

I AM THE GREEN GOBLIN

Today is the day I will take over the world. I am tired of Spider-Man winning. All of my plans to take over, he has done this all of my life.

I plan to meet him this afternoon to kill him once and for all. I get my sharp spears and start to shoot them at Spider-Man.

However, somehow it doesn't work. My plans have been ruined once again. One day, I will get my way and take over the world once and for all.

Callum McDoanld (12)

Trinity Academy Halifax, Holmfield

WRONGED

I'm James Hook, otherwise known as Captain Hook. I'm that huge, fearsome pirate you're all afraid of, right? No! You're wrong.

Or maybe your all-time favourite character, Peter Pan, is the villain you never suspected! Have you considered that he forced a crocodile to attack me? Bite. My. Hand. Off! No? Don't you remember those terrible times when Peter Pan mocked me, provoked me, pretended he was a pirate to deceive me? Wouldn't you hate if that happened to you? Father was the terror of the seas; I just wanted to make him feel proud. But do I feel proud?

Ruby-Jo Starkey (11)
Weaverham High School, Weaverham

LIKE ROMEO AND JULIET

They believe I'm a villain. I just didn't want him to be without me. You must understand, I was obsessed, deeply infatuated with this beautiful, complex being. I constantly yearned to discover every inch of his body, despite the pain he'd caused me.

He had ripped out my heart with mere words. Rejection. They call it petty teenage rejection but I had never felt such pain before. How was I supposed to know peace?

Chanae Mcdonald (16)
Winchmore School, Winchmore Hill

YoungWriters®
Est. 1991

YOUNG WRITERS INFORMATION

We hope you have enjoyed reading this book – and that you will continue to in the coming years.

If you're a young writer who enjoys reading and creative writing, or the parent of an enthusiastic poet or story writer, do visit our website **www.youngwriters.co.uk**. Here you will find free competitions, workshops and games, as well as recommended reads, a poetry glossary and our blog. There's lots to keep budding writers motivated to write!

If you would like to order further copies of this book, or any of our other titles, then please give us a call or order via your online account.

Young Writers
Remus House
Coltsfoot Drive
Peterborough
PE2 9BF
(01733) 890066
info@youngwriters.co.uk

Join in the conversation!
Tips, news, giveaways and much more!

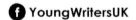 YoungWritersUK  YoungWritersCW 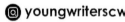 youngwriterscw